Pretend
We
Live
Here

First printing: August 2018
Paperback ISBN 978-1-892061-82-9
(limited edition hardcover ISBN 978-1-892061-84-3)

Front cover design by Jess Vande Werken
Photo by Elena Kendall-Aranda
Back cover by Olivia Croom
Interior layout by Tyler Meese

Future Tense Books
PO Box 42416
Portland, OR 97242
futuretensebooks.com

Future Tense Books are distributed by Small Press Distribution
spdbooks.org and Ingram

Pretend
We
Live
Here

Stories

Genevieve Hudson

Future Tense Books
portland, oregon

"She wanted to be extraordinary, to possess a savage glitter."
—Joy Williams, *The Quick and the Dead*

God
Hospital

My tooth has gone black. Mother said it died from sugar and my forgetful brushing and now I must suffer the consequences. She says it kindly, but it lands hot as the truth because there's nothing she can do. We don't have health insurance, and even if we did, dental is never included. So, here I am sucking on a popsicle, the only thing that soothes it, in the God-awful August sun and watching Duris and waiting for Curly to come take us to the healer.

Watermelon Road is peaceful this morning. Television comes through the neighbor's trailers, all rattle and hum. Surrounding the Estates is a high blue sky and a clump of skinny dogwood trees and a field of brown grass. When the wind hits the grass, sometimes I smell sugar. Other times I smell clay, all slick and mineral. The fence that separates our homes from the thirsty pasture behind us is sun-rotted and bug-eaten. It wouldn't keep a thing in or a thing out.

Duris gallops the yard in front of our homes slathering sunscreen on her skin even though it doesn't matter because she's burned crawdad-red already from a weekend spent at Lake Lurleen. Her legs are all muscle and kick. She does the robot across the raw dirt driveway, dances to the music in her own mind. Her hair is smooth and butter-colored, and she is a beauty even when she is bored. Especially when she is bored.

"He's fixing to be here any minute. My M-A-N," Duris spells it out like it's a bad word.

"I'm waiting," I say.

I hold the portable electric fan to my face and close my eyes. The air is thick and yeasty. You could fry an egg on the sidewalk. I wouldn't dare walk my bare feet across the pavement. I spit, and it sizzles pink with blood. My toes are painted the same shimmering sad color as my popsicle, and I am just admiring them when I hear Curly's truck. My tooth buzzes in my gum. I've seen Curly at a distance—greasy black hair and eyes yellow as cat fur. Now I'm going to meet him in real life because here he comes up the drive past the line of postboxes. I lick soft sugar from the blue-stained popsicle stick and watch his truck fart out black clouds of pollution.

Duris hoots when she sees Curly and smacks her thigh in glee. He hoists her into his thick arms, and they perform a scene of spinning around and making noises. Her braid comes undone and spills like hay onto her skinny red shoulders. He carries her toward me. Her legs wrap around his core, and she screams with a joy I've never known.

I hand Curly a bag of turnips, deep mean green, for his help and he chunks it in the back of the trunk and thanks me. I'm bringing a bag for the healer.

Curly is unlike the other boys we know, in age, yes, but also in life experience. The Air Force took him to the desert where he jumped out of fighter planes and saved babies from tragic deaths and killed terrorists. He was shot three times in the neck and never did die, and people say he's a hero. He's alive now because of the blessing he got from the healer. The healer might be a prophet. The healer might also have a direct line to God.

Curly's truck is spotless inside and out. That's proof of his purity. He opens the door like a gentleman and picks me up with big calloused hands and sets me down right on the back seat. The red stripe on Curly's neck is puckered and pink at the edges and swollen to the size of an earthworm. Under the stripe once lived three bullets.

I hold my hand to my mouth when I talk to hide my black fang, which is in the front of my mouth.

"Go on and let me see it."

I shake my head. I don't want to show him my plum-colored teeth.

"If I'm fixing to take you to heal it, I need to get a good, long look."

I've run out of home remedies. Duris's maw brewed a tea of egg yolk and chopped mint leaves that she swore would fix the sting. She had me swirl safflower oil around my mouth for 20 minutes first thing each morning then spit it out in the toilet. She grew turmeric bulbs in a smelly plot of dirt near the radiator out back and ground them into a salve, but nothing helped it. I still wake every morning with blood stains on my pillowcase. I think of my mother, toothless as a chicken and so lonely, and I think I'll do anything to end up different.

I remove my hand and Curly levels his eyes into mine and drags his gaze down to my mouth. Five more are turning gray in the back. He nods solemnly and leans in to get a better look. He assures me the healer can fix it no problem. His face, structurally speaking, is beautiful. It is a face that reveals the skull beneath it. Skin pulled tight to show the sunken eye sockets. It is a face that says bone and mandible and chin. There is the tiniest wing tattooed on his temple. I almost think he's wearing eyeliner, but he's not. He's so good looking it scares the shit out of me.

Curly grips my chin so he can study the inside of my mouth. I close my eyes and imagine that he is taking me to Lake Lurleen with him and not to the healer. I've never been to a dock like the one he took Duris to, but I have stood on the tan necks of the cliffs that line the green lake and jumped into the swirling warmth below. Curly's friend owns a summer home out there, and when his friend was out of town he brought Duris. The house was doll-like and haunted and covered with clean carpet, and giant beach towels hung from the back of every door. They pretended they lived there, ate cocktail shrimp from a bucket and drank tomato juice and sucked the guts from limes. They sat in a rowboat tied to the mooring and emptied airplane-sized vodka bottles into their throats and dreamed they could fly away or sail away or anything away. Duris explained how they pulled the American flag down from its pole on the front porch and laid it on the grass and went all the way. Duris said: *It must be how the rich live.* That's when Curly told her he knew how to find the God Hospital and that he'd been there himself.

I imagine myself lying on the flag with Curly. I imagine him rolling over onto his back, his heart beating fast under his raw, sun-burned ribs and winking at me and saying, "Yeah, baby, I'll take you to the healer." I imagine him right now, leaning in, kissing me and my nasty mouth and liking every second of it. Though I guess at 13, I'm too young for that.

GREENS
FO SIL⇨

Reads the sign right in front of our driveway. Mother nailed it to a tree so you can see it from the main road. Mother and I keep a garden where collard heads and kale stalks reach toward the power lines and tomatoes grow fat and leak their innards out. Mother's hands are slow with the watering can and slow with the picking, so she needs me. We're passing the garden now in Curly's truck. No one's there, and it looks deserted. Sometimes I find Mother in the garden moving her mouth likes she's talking to someone I can't see. When she notices me, she looks startled, like she needs to find a place for my face and when she does find it, where I fit in her life, her whole memory comes crumbling back, and she looks sad.

I yank the greens fresh for each of our customers and hand them over in used Piggly Wiggly plastic bags. One day, I think, we could expand our greens selling business and move to a store in town or purchase a stall at the farmer's market on the college campus. The college people like getting greens with soil still on the stems. It makes them feel real in a world made mostly of plastic and propane.

If they knew we were out here growing them and picking them ourselves, I bet we'd have a line to the Florida border.

Curly's truck smells like gas. I have been reading about pollution, the receding glaciers in Greenland, the mass deaths of penguins on beaches in Alaska, the graves of 100 wolves in Alaska, and I know that these sick and sputtering engines are part of the problem. I know that everything is connected. Driving cars that purr like deranged cats and cough out foul smells is causing our planet to get hot as hellfire. But you can't get around driving in Alabama. You need a car to go anywhere. Walking would take hours and buses do not exist. Duris does not want to understand the pollution situation. I've tried to explain it. She refuses to see a connection. Spraying hair through an aerosol nozzle inside a sealed room couldn't possibly affect a country far away whose name she can't remember. Mud-riding through a dry creek bed couldn't remove snow from the top of a mountain or fatten the surface of the sea so that it spills onto shores where it shouldn't.

But I believe it can, even if I can't explain it in proper scientific terms. I believe we are part of something bigger than what we can see.

Curly grabs himself a lump of chew and sticks it beneath his lip. He starts to rant about how in the military everyone has health insurance, but civilians shouldn't expect a handout like that. People need to be resourceful or get a goddamn job.

"You don't deserve nothing," he says, training that chilly gaze onto me in the backseat. "Not you as in you but you as in all of us.

Problem is that people don't work anymore. They just expect handouts."

I think of my Mother's trembling hands, the mind that reaches for memories in a fog so dense she's not sure what's there. The house she grew up in had asbestos in the ceiling boards and black mold under the floor, but her brain mostly survived that. She went crazy after my daddy disappeared, a Puerto Rican farmer who I've seen in exactly one picture, and she began to eat long strips of lead-laced paint from the walls until her eyes crossed and she was never quite the same. People say he was kidnapped, but no one tells me the whole story. She can't have a real job, but she loves to work a garden. We had to move next to Duris and her maw when I was just a babe. We get checks in the mail each month, but they're so small we have to stretch and stretch and stretch them.

"Well that's not Christian," says Duris. I know she says it because she would like to go to the doctor and have her athlete's foot investigated, but she doesn't have insurance either. "God's supposed to give. Doesn't he think we should all have enough to eat and stuff like that? I am not Christian or nothing. I'm just saying."

A sour straw dangles from her glossed mouth and Curly looks at her and laughs and yanks the straw from her perfect white teeth and swallows the thing whole. His laugh is an explosion. He flings his whole head back, showing us the black hair on his neck and the fresh pimples around the scar.

"God helps those that help themselves," says Curly.

Duris thinks this is hilarious and ruffles through her bag for more candy. She barely eats real food. She takes down Sour Patch

Kids and sour rings and off-brand gummy bears. She never gets cavities because her genes are superior. She offers me a pink ring crusted in sugar.

"No thanks."

That much sugar sizzles the tooth root.

I can see Duris's reflection in the side mirror, and it makes me jealous. I look away. Duris is the kind of beauty that would be beautiful anywhere, even in New York City. She's the kind of beauty that will one day attract the attention of one of the modeling agents to whom she sends dozens of Walmart portraits with the words YOURS written in cursive purple marker across the bottom and sprayed with a puff of Wild GRRL No. 7. The agent will consider her strong jawline, the wide mouth, the cold marble eyes placed almost too close together. He will swoop her up for his own fortunes. He will take her to Paris where she will model with Europeans, get felt up in back rooms by debauched French men, eat expensive cheese, smile on the cover of big magazines. He will scrub the R-dropping Southern accent from her tongue. I will pick up the magazines in line at Winn-Dixie and point to her upturned nose, say, *That's my cousin!*

At least that is how it goes in our visualizing. Our visualizing is an important part of how we manifest the lives we want. Duris visualizes for fifteen minutes each morning, and she has me visualize for her, too. We don't focus on what could happen to me in our visualizing because we are attending to her first, and I don't mind. My dreams aren't as big as Duris's. I just want my tooth fixed. She wants shimmer and fame and hundred-dollar sunglasses. She wants people to approach her with trays of twinkling drinks and give her small, exquisite boxes and ask for her autograph.

I would be happy to stay here at the Eutaw Mobile Home Estates and take care of Mother and read every book in the county library and help tend to the modest ring of trailer homes and scatter seeds in my garden. So, we're different.

Duris is my second cousin. Blood-related but barely. Her maw appreciates my influence. She watches me iron bed sheets on the porch, walk the grass cutter through the weeds that live between our houses, read books that the high school assigns and even books it doesn't. *Books.* All those stories. So many stories. They take me to places far away that I won't ever go.

Curly continues to tell us how God Hospitals like the one we're going to will soon be an alternative to conventional health care. He tells us that people have only had access to health care as we know it for the last couple of years. It's spoiling us. His granddaddy lived to be 98 and was quick as a whip and strong as a bull until the day he died and never, not even one time, stepped foot inside a doctor's office. Curly drives slowly, signals before he turns, signals before he overtakes cars.

I wonder what Curly means by *health care as we know it*? I've been to the doctor on a few occasions. I can count them all on one hand: dog bite, strep throat, blood in the ear. Each time, I had to curl up and sleep in the sticky ER seats and wait for 10 hours to be seen by a man who looked at me with absent eyes and touched me with gloved hands for 15 minutes before he handed Mother a piece of yellow paper and a $700 bill for facility fees.

I don't ask Duris or Curly why this man would agree to heal me for nothing at all in return except a bag of fresh turnips. Maybe part of me hasn't asked on purpose.

The windows are down, and I smell cow dung and summer rain as we push deeper into the woods. Curly turns up the radio and the syrupy voice of Tammy Wynette is among us.

The drive is bumpy, and the road is unpaved, and the trees we pass are crooked and half-dead. I don't know what's killing the trees, but they've gone dark as oil at the roots, and their bark pulls off in long sheets, and their limbs are without leaf.

The healer is almost famous. Even the college kids who ride around on bicycles and have telephones on their wrists know about him. In the rumors I've heard, his hair is long and tangled and feral. He lives in a trailer that's spray-painted with the word JESUS in all capital letters in red paint on the side. One rumor: not paint, but blood.

One rumor: sleeps on the roof at night and makes love to God on the full moon.

One rumor: bathes in chicken guts in a tub in his front yard.

One rumor: killed his twin brother and buried him beneath his trailer.

One rumor: is sweet and kind and after he lays his hands on you, you will never get sick again, never be sad, never, never.

One rumor: was once a tax accountant and now is simply crazy with no magic to speak of and don't go near him.

Part of me wants to ask Curly how he knows where to find the healer. Part of me wonders why Curly is taking me at all. Probably it has to do with Duris and her beauty. Duris and her beauty have opened many doors for her, and on account of our blood relation, they will now open a door for me. For a long time, I did not understand why Duris spent time with me. I thought: she's bored or has nothing better to do. I thought: we are the only girls of similar age that live at Eutaw Mobile Homes estate. I thought: that's how family does it. I thought: she is lonely.

We pass a garden of white crosses written on with black paint. White crosses are suddenly everywhere I look. They are stuck deep into the soil and covered in apocalyptic sayings like: HELL WILL BURN BURN BURN YOU.

Curly says, "Here we go now. Getting close."

Jesus SAVES

REPENT GARDEN

READ THE BIBLE

TOO LATE IN HELL FIRE WATER

The water in hell to DRINK is HOT HOT HOT

JESUS GOD SEX SINNERS

Sex Pit Help Me Jesus

GOD HOSPITAL

Crosses are painted on tree trunks and broken fence boards and on weather-worn flags and rotting planks that have been nailed to the side of anything or held in place with rusted barbed wire. Crosses grow out of the green bushes. Crosses come out of the green grass and the green weeds and the green ivy that grows over it all. So many crosses. In my eyes, there are only crosses.

"Well Goddamn," whispers Duris, solemn, like she's just entered church.

"Now, now," says Curly. "Don't let it scare you."

When we pull up to the God Hospital, the sky is burnt orange and too bright to look at straight on. And sure as shit there's the letters J-E-S-U-S graffiti-ed in red right across the trailer. The JESUS paint dripped, and I can see where it ran toward the ground before the sun baked the word into place. This word is not alone. The entire trailer is covered in Biblical scrawl just like the crosses we saw on the road. Crosses dominate his yard, too, as do bike tires and lawn furniture and old freezers and antique lamps and broken doll houses. Sculptures. Whatever he could find. Busted television sets. Transistor radios. Stereo systems. Garden hoses. Motorcycles. Dead cars. Mattresses. Everything. There is a white leather armchair with a slit down the center gushing out yellow innards, and jesusjesusjesusjesus is scribbled across it in black marker. The biggest sign says:

WELCOME TO GOD'S HOSPITAL. ALL Y'ALL WELCOME.

The healer's got a different kind of trailer than our homes, which could pass as real houses with their well-made front porches and plastic paneling that smells like wood. The carpet inside our homes is chemical clean, and the windows are large and have shutters painted a deep dark blue. But there is something sharp and sinister about the healer's place, like glass that catches the light and glints.

The healer, or at least it must be the healer, steps onto the porch and folds his arms over a long white dress, leans against the door frame, and tips the brim of a broad straw hat. Duris wants to come into the trailer with us, but Curly tells her to stay put. Maybe he thinks Duris isn't brave enough to handle this. Maybe he wants it to be just the two of us having this experience. Either way, Duris sits in the car as Curly leads me to the stairs. I look back a few times at Duris. Her mouth frowns just a touch and her wild eyes are quiet. I'm terrified and close to saying let's go back, but I feel it's too late already and my mouth won't form the request. Duris makes herself smile, and I know she doesn't know what to do. I squeeze my eyes tight. Curly's hand is on my back, and he applies a little pressure, telling me, without telling me, to go forth.

A pipe snakes through the dead grass and dribbles water from its mouth into a smelly puddle of mud. We walk through a swarm of fuck bugs, through a wall of wet heat, through the prophetic damning sculpture garden. The healer holds us in his gaze the entire time. We step onto the first stair, and I'm not scared anymore. Long, greasy hair runs down the healer's neck and mixes with the coiled hair on his chest. He smiles at me with rows of perfect teeth. His teeth are pure and good. I wonder if Duris is visualizing. What is she visualizing? What future does she see for me?

Curly and the healer hug each other like brothers. What I'm saying is they embrace in a real way, not a slap of the back and a *no homo man*. It can't be true, but I think Curly kisses the healer right on his dry pink lips. Curly says Duris will wait in the truck, but that he's going come in with me. I try to hide my smile. He wants it to be just us. He doesn't want me to be afraid.

"She look like a prophet," says the healer.

I think he means my shaved head, which Mother sheared to peach fuzz after I got lice. I like it so much I want to keep it short like this, even though people at school have been calling me a *monk*.

Inside, the healer asks me if I want coffee. I hate coffee and say so but I do it politely, and the healer has tea. Curly admires the Jesus Altar, which is decorated with golden chimes and copper crosses and framed pictures of Paul the Apostle and Christ. Rosaries dangle from every hook or edge. There are framed pictures of other people, too. Strangers to me, but not to the healer. The altar takes up an entire wall, and there is the same scriptural scrawl of GOD HOSPITAL written above the altar on a piece of river wood. I should be scared. I do know this. I know it in my brain, but my heart is on a different path. My heart wants to trust just one thing, and this might be it. The healer stirs sugar into a teacup of black liquid and smiles at me.

The healer, who introduces himself as Dove, walks me out the back door and I hear an engine start up and my blood runs backward and cold. Is Duris driving away? She might try to start a scene and make Curly leave to check on her. No. It idles. Music starts in the truck again. Duris only wanted to play music. There's Tammy W. again, and the sad-sadness comes radiating toward us in the backyard, and even Dove stops and closes his eyes in reference to "Stand by Your Man." He begins singing under his breath.

The light is soft and spilling through the trees around us. It's the thin, magic afternoon color that turns everything yellow. Golden hour. We step into that golden light and move toward what looks like a metal intake table with two chairs on either side. Dove pulls

22

his mouth into a smile and gestures for me to sit. I give him the bag of greens, and he looks pleased. He puts them on the ground.

A river runs close to here. I picture it winding its way through the thick forest, people I know stuck into fat rubber inner tubes, popping open beers and letting their mutts run along the river's edge beside them. I can almost hear them laughing though I know that's impossible.

"You come here for the healing," Dove says kindly.

We are sitting on lawn chairs pulled right up to the edge of the table. I have taken a cup of tea though I don't drink it. I just hold it between my thighs. Curly walks around the yard kind of nervous with his hands in his pockets. His eyes shift over all the Jesus junk like he's looking for something. I don't even know Curly. His beauty could be one of those tricks Duris's maw warns about.

"Tell me about your symptoms. What's ailing you?"

I tell him about the screaming pain that won't relent. It keeps waking me at night. I tell how I don't want to eat and how I'm afraid to smile because of the way it looks. I tell him there's a smell, too, like greens that've gone to rot.

Dove stirs his cup with a tiny spoon and listens. Mmmhmmm goes his mouth. He nods like he understands and knows just what is wrong. He tells me how God healed him from a calloused cluster of ear cysts that made him deaf as a dog. He tells me how since the healing he's been blessed with an ability to mend others and a willingness to do the dirty work of medicine that others are afraid of doing. He says he does it for free. It's what the Lord wants.

"Like pulling teeth?" I ask.

"For instance," says Dove. "Don't be afraid, baby. The Lord is here."

Dove crosses his legs in his dress, which might not be a dress but a primitive tunic. There is something feminine about the gangly hand he brings to his mouth each time he sips his coffee. There's something feral about the smooth muscles that run through his limbs. I trust him. I don't know why.

Dove begins to tell me how he was given a vision from the Lord that he needed to start his own God Hospital right here where people could get healed for free. He has patients come each week. Most are successful, and they depart happy and smiling and alive. He blesses them before they go with special God water that bubbles up naturally from the ground right beneath our feet. When he says *most leave alive*, I feel a coolness rise up on my arms.

Dove stands from the intake table and gestures for me to follow him. He takes me farther into his property and into a clearing. He asks me to lay on what looks like a dental chair. Curly stands beside us, almost like one of those nurses you see on television. The tarp under the chair is flecked with dried brown material. Dove gives me a small Jesus figure to hold during the process.

"In case it gets to hurting," he says.

Dove pulls up a bucket of wrenches sitting in a teal liquid. It smells like bleach. Crows flap their wings through the sky. I close my eyes and visualize Duris wondering if she should come check on me. I visualize her hand in mine, and I wonder how bad a row of black teeth really is. I ask the God inside of my mind if this is okay and then listen for an answer.

"I'm going to let you be," says Curly. "Like. Give you some privacy. I'll check on Duris. She's using up too much gas running the engine like that. Going to kill the car and then we'll never be able to leave."

He makes a nervous laughing sound and waves his arms around like a bird caught in a fight with the wind.

"Five more minutes," I say, like a question. "Five more minutes then we'll go together."

I want to ask Curly if I can hold his hand or if he can sit down with me while Dove operates, but he's walking away already. He never even looks to make sure the tools aren't rusted, and that everything is okay.

I close my eyes again, and I think I hear a voice say: *leave.*

Dove says all he has to do is pull a few of the bad molars out and then give me a tea to drink. New teeth will grow in pure and white and never rotten. He smiles his pearly, perfect fangs and he says: "I used to have rows of cavities, man. You can trust me. Trust me, baby doll."

I grab the Jesus doll's head and squeeze, preparing for the pain. I wonder if I should tell Dove I have to go to the bathroom, but then what? I imagine myself anywhere different which helps calm a person when they're about to experience a traumatic event. I think of the how the soil feels between my fingers when I dig in the garden at the Eutaw Mobile Homes Estate. I picture pulling the green, fibrous spines of collards from the dirt and how they smell of sulfur and stink in a way that's noble. I imagine the sun on my neck and my back bent over the little patch of earth I love.

When I look up at Dove, he's eclipsed the sun. His face is blocking out its perfect circle of light. It glows behind him like a gloriole. When I study his eyes, I see a single wet drop run down his cheek. His tear hits me right in the chest. I visualize Duris again. I try to manifest her help, and then I hear her voice call my name. It is a melody, like she isn't even scared, like I shouldn't be either.

"Wait," she says. She's on the back porch, and Dove looks up, and so do I. She looks younger than I've ever seen her look. "Get on up, Rae," she says. "Get on up, girl."

But I'm already standing. My legs are beneath me, my bare feet bracing into wet soil. The chair is no place for my body. I hear Curly rev the engine of his truck, but all I see is Duris. She squares her shoulders. She flips her hair over her shoulder like some kind of splendid horse. She is filled with light. All the light that the sun can give has flooded her. Her skin is stitched in gold. She reaches out her hand, and I'm already walking toward her. It's not even far.

Date
Book

November, say they, is the cruelest month. Don't believe them. It's hot July with her bike grease, her stringless flings, her flat tires, her tendinitis of the wrist. The sun burns us right in the face. Neither of us has seen Sonoma, a dyke march, City Lights Books, or each other before. Everything, even our breath, boils. Cruelty is meeting someone and knowing what you want is time. I take your hand at the farmer's market to lead you through the lines. The trick is letting go. "Tijuana," I say. "You'll have to tell me about."

August holds possibility, like a baptism, your itinerary through town, and the Polaroid we find of someone else's fun. *The strawberries here taste like sugar*. It's a promise. But you are from better places, where water is greener than trees and the sky is bluer than the milk of your iris. Your fields are on fire with the red of them, the berries you smear your fingers through. I can't stop eating the vine. Train songs will always remind me of you.

By September you are another country again. The thought of you causes me to pick weeds, to put poems on the back of receipt paper. I get a package in the mail. It's wrapped in a map of the place where you live. I fall in love with the smell of the cardboard, the image of your palms folding the top down. We meet on an island in the middle. I feed myself to you until we're full.

October is for dressing up, for getting robbed. I call you not crying. Someone breaks into my room. They touch my bed. They leave the smell of skin and clattered coins. I can't stop thinking about the stories on my computer I didn't save. The essay I was writing about you. Behind your back, I can make you into whatever I want. Your voice handles crisis better than anyone. You have mastered the art using a thousand words to say nothing. I fall into the receiver; it's hard plastic I am beginning to regard as your cheek. I go to the bookstore and flirt so hard five people try to kiss me.

November is not cruel but filled with visits. I wake up dreaming. You're in my mind. You sleep later than I like, and I pretend I am sleeping, too. You introduce me to your friends, and I practice saying hello in the mirror until my cheeks fall down. I memorize your dialect, the cutting away of consonance, and the inflections that leave your mouth. Your mouth meets my mouth, and we both like what happens.

December and we're standing on your parents' dock in Nanaimo in our underwear. You are playing a mix tape on your iPhone. They are the same songs we've listened to 988 times but they still sound new like everything about you always does. You dare me to jump in, but you do it first. Nothing scares you except maybe me. I follow you under the freezing water, and our breath is snatched from our chests. "It's fucking ice," we say, and our laughter becomes clouds.

January.

In February we go to Seattle to say goodbye. We accidentally rent a weekend apartment over a lesbian bar. We laugh all the way up the stairs. Capitol Hill is all noise, but we don't even hear it. We never go to the lesbian bar. We've made our own lesbian bar in the kitchen. We pretend we live here. We drink from cups. We unmake the bed. We note the Space Needle in the window. We pour white wine from cartons. We do everything we've never done before and everything we have. You tell me stories, and I listen. I want you to keep going. Keep going. You say you've never met anyone like me, which sounds familiar, like I've heard it before. You say a lot of things. Keep going.

I drive you to the ferry. It's so early it's nighttime. I am sweating from my coffee. You can smell me. My favorite place to rest my hand is on your thigh, so I do it. I point at the flag on the boat that's yours. It's going to carry you. You'll be home in a few hours, working again at the crisis line where you shepherd other people out of sadness.

Too Much Is Never Enough

When I was young, I dreamt I was a boy. A Disney prince like the kind found in *Aladdin* and *The Lion King*. Charming, and boisterous, and able to get the girl. I ran around the house with a wooden sword tucked into my belt. I jumped onto rugs as if they were magic carpets that could fly under my feet. I prowled the creek behind my house like a wild dog. Dads in the neighborhood confused me for their sons, and it felt like I had won a prize. In the mirror, a boy stared back. I fell asleep once, and while I slept, I did have a magic carpet, and I did have a boy's body, and I was so happy you would have thought it was Christmas morning and all the presents under the tree were for me. But when I woke up, the magic carpet was only a rug, and I was just a girl.

Catherine Elizabeth was my best friend. Most people called her Cat Liz, but I called her the Lizard, and she called me the Snake. The Lizard and the Snake were the stars of our own adventures.

We twisted plots in our favor. The Lizard wore dresses, but she still knew how to climb a tree and cross a creek. She seemed really comfortable in her dresses. She said they gave her more room to move. I cut a deal with my mom that I only had to wear a dress one Sunday a month to church. I could wear jeans all other Sundays. We both thought we were getting the short stick. I already had this strange sensation that the clothes I wore could change my life. For instance, during the dress days I only ate one donut during coffee hour. But during my jean-wearing days I could eat two. Maybe more. I could eat everything.

By accident I discovered that if I laid on my back and put my feet in the air, I could make my vagina fart. I wanted to see if the Lizard could do it, too. Turns out she could. We spent an entire afternoon farting from our vaginas. This same afternoon, the Lizard's mom came in to see if we wanted a snack of fruit leather and Pecan Sandies. Admittedly, it was the wrong time for the mother to enter the scene. The Lizard and I were putting our vaginas against each other and farting into each other. We thought it was hilarious. A joke that we could tell the other with our bodies. We were eight. It was harmless. But looking back now, I can see why the Lizard's mom freaked out.

After the farting incident, the Lizard stopped being available to hang out. Her mom was still nice to me, but she rarely let me stay for dinner anymore, and the Lizard was suddenly enrolled in Ballet Saturday, which was during our normal hang time. The Lizard dropped the Liz at school and started going by Katie. There were already so many Katies at our school. She became lost in a chorus of Katies. If I called her name, ten heads would turn. I couldn't find her anymore. Maybe she liked it: feeling that she was just one of the girls.

The Lizard's place was not vacant for long. I needed someone to fill the friendship-sized hole in my heart, and that's when I met Mason. Mason looked like an angel, which was lucky for him because he acted like the devil so the two just about evened themselves out. Mason's eyes were blue as rainwater. His dove-white curls literally flounced. This is how Mason got away with it. It being everything.

When I met Mason, he told me he had figured out how to build a bomb from an AA battery and skateboard bearings. The bomb did not work. But it's the thought that counts. Mason had a rifle under his bed that he swore wasn't loaded, but when he pointed it in my face, I almost vomited on my Ninja Turtles T-shirt. His dad would take him hunting the one weekend out of the year they saw each other. Mason had the smooth buck antlers to prove it. A picture on his wall showed him smeared in dark blood holding the head of an animal to his chest. The jet-black eyes of the deer had gone glassy with death. Its pink tongue was the only thing that looked alive.

My mom thought Mason was a delight. He said *yes ma'am* and ate her steamed broccoli and more than anything he had the aura of a lost puppy who needed his ears scratched. Mason was exactly what a boy should be. I tried to laugh like him: that silent guffaw that shook his shoulders so cutely. We already dressed similarly, but I was taking notes. He wore white undershirts with the necks stretched and subtle dirt stains down the front. A fishhook was pierced through the bill of his ball cap. My heart went swollen when I looked at him. We were the same height, same weight, same shape. When we wrestled, I could pin him down first. His body wriggled beneath me. He hated to be beaten by a girl. I hated to be beaten by a girl, too.

Mason stole a pack of his mother's cigarettes, and that's how I smoked my first Marlboro. We went behind his house and down through the gulley littered with teenage trash from teenage parties. He didn't like his mother smoking, which is why he took those packs from her, but Mason said as long as we had them, we might as well use them. The most exciting part about smoking was the wet filter. It never got more intimate than that: our spit touching on the same cottony tube. It was like kissing him with something in between. We shared the soggy cigarette until I coughed something yellow onto my shoes. We arm wrestled on a tree stump, and I thought about letting him win. The light had gone weak pink at the sky's edge, and the sun was poised just above the maples, ready to sink under the Earth. At the last second, I used the full force of my bicep to level his arm down on my winning side. When he shook his hand out, his knuckles were flecked with blood and bark.

During my friendship with Mason, my dreams got even more confusing. I wanted Mason to be my Jasmine, but only if Jasmine could be a boy and I could be a boy, too. I wanted to wear Mason's undershirts with their subtle stains down the front. I wanted him to hug my arm while he wore the same shirt. I wanted boyish perfection, and I wanted that boyish perfection to love me. Mason was sent away to military camp before we turned 13. I saw him during the summers after that. His body continued to grow, and so did mine. We no longer had the same height, same weight, same shape. He stayed a lanky, boyish thing, just a bigger version of it. His voice deepened until it sounded like he was growling when he spoke. He carried pistols on his belt, and an army crew cut replaced his flouncy curls. My body had started a deceit that it never stopped. I left those skateboard lines behind and filled out in places I wanted to hide under baggy jeans and tough black T-shirts. When Mason was 19, he died in a hotel room after being released from rehab. A needle was stuck deep in his elbow. His boyish body was put in a casket, and we buried it in the softest dirt. I still dream about him. He is on our magic carpet. He is riding it forever.

The part of the story I haven't told you yet is that Mason and the Lizard fell in love. It happened one summer when he was home from military school. There was something they found in each other they could never find in me. I was not enough boy for the Lizard. Not enough girl for Mason. I was something in between them. I was both too much and not enough. Mason and the Lizard now called Katie would drop acid on the shores of a dirty dammed up lake just outside of town and escape their minds together. I will resist the magic carpet metaphor here and instead tell you that they really liked each other. I never spent time with the two of them together, which looking back seems strange. But I heard about their summer. They each said I reminded them of the other. I was there, even when I was not.

When I think of my childhood now, I don't remember myself as a girl or even as Aladdin. I think of myself as Mason, who is actually a dead boy. There is something sick about that. About imagining yourself as a dead boy. What is a dead boy if not a boy who never dies? I imagine Mason as the man I never could be, but also as the man he never could be. Because he never was. When I picture him now he is always laughing. He is laughing silently under those curls that were supposed to let us get away with everything but never actually helped us get away with anything at all.

Woman Without a Memory

I met a woman without a memory once. She had a face like Kentucky and a laugh like gin. She would dip her golden finger in my water. She would tell me: *drink*. And I would drink, and she would forget.

This woman had a talent for twerking. She would twerk to Drake's "One Dance," and occasionally people would fall in love with the way she spun her body like it was for them when it wasn't. She ate pizza rolls and vegan pasta and walked two hours up a hill to a hospital in the forest so she could ride the air tram down.

One day, she took me with her to the air tram. We hiked through a thick wood where the moss grew on the north side of the trees. I didn't know you could use moss as a compass until she told me. She put her face to the fur and breathed.

Even without a memory, she knew how to get home.

In the air tram, we flew over the rooftops like witches. This is what she wanted to show me: a river full of poison fish and rusted machines and other people's urine. The Cascade mountains with their teeth and curve. They bent into a horizon and bit the blue vein of sky. Under us, river apartments jagged across the bank with sunroofs cleaved open. I wondered about the people on the balcony whose windows always faced the rain.

The woman without a memory made up stories about people who washed their hair with vodka and lived in rooms with bed bugs and came out to sleep on cool slabs of river rock and shiver.

For someone with no memory, she knew how to tell a good story.

A few days after the air tram, I visited a store for witches. The shelves were filled with smooth jade stones, jags of white rock, a crystal hued in purple that thrummed when I ran my hand above it. There were shelves of spells that you could cast on yourself and other people. The witch who worked there kept two teeth pressed to the outside of her bottom lip. She placed her palms on the heft of her belly, said: *hold here*. She showed me how to grip myself. She told me everyone has a pendulum inside them. She demonstrated how to feel the slight sway of a body and how to ask it yes and how to hear no.

It was the Fourth of July. I hated that holiday. The city smattered the sky with color. Reds smeared across the black until the air steamed. Loud noises and the animals were afraid. We were on a roof. The view was supposed to stun us, but I was staring at the woman without a memory. I took videos of her singing Shania Twain and Reba McEntire. She screamed "Independence Day!" at the top of her lungs and the city didn't listen.

I texted her the video a few days later and she texted back, *Thanks, Dan*, as if that were my name, as if my name were a secret between us—a memory maybe.

The woman came with me to get a tattoo. I put an eye on the back of my arm so I could see what was coming.

After the tattoo, I dropped the woman off in my red truck, and she said, "Please don't try to kiss me."

It was almost like she remembered.

When she left town, I placed my hands on my pendulum, and I listened.

Yes or No.

I really couldn't tell.

The woman without a memory burned a line across the continent. She was going east. She would drink from the Mississippi. She would park under a tree in Utah. She would take a picture of each rest stop and forget to send them to me.

Where would she end up? I asked her this, but she couldn't remember.

The more the woman forgot, the more I didn't.

Memory was all I had. I lived in a house of memory. I slipped drapes of memory through my window rods. I laid floorboards of memory one plank at a time. I scrubbed dust from my bookshelves so they shone with memory. I built staircases of memory that led to bedrooms of memory. I made a balcony of memory where I could sunbathe in memory.

I imagined the woman driving into the desert and bracing her face against the sharp sun. I imagined her bleached by all that bright white heat.

I was in Moab once so I pictured this woman there, too. A strange place. I saw a long road kicked up with dust. There were wooden structures brimming with turquoise jewelry and copper spoons. The restaurants served eggs and acai bowls, and the men were mean-faced with sand under their nails. They liked to growl at the birds and bark at the cats to scare them. The air was so dry in Utah, my lips chapped when I stepped outside. The desert scraped me clean for the first time. It singed the sin away. Nothing could rot there. Nothing could decay.

I walked through a field of needles. The spindles of stone all looked the same. The hot wind burrowed into my skin and changed me.

I imagined the woman stepping through whipped dunes of red sand. It might feel like home. It might feel like *no pressure really*.

I bought a crystal from the witch's store to give to the woman. I bought a box of spells. The crystal was ice-white, and when I held it to my forehead, I felt it in my jaw. I wanted the crystal to remind her of something. I wanted it to stretch her aura pink at its edges. I wanted its true, tender color to show.

I went to a basement where a psychic rubbed sage beneath my feet, and the smoke's tendrils curled up my calves. The psychic asked me to call in my ancestors, my spirit guides, the ghost of someone gone. She put out the sage like a cigarette. I thought I heard my great-grandmother calling me from a convent in San Juan. The psychic drew a card from her deck and said, "Uh oh, honey." And I almost knew what she meant.

Holes

My nurse's English is bad, but my Dutch is even worse. Every four hours she comes to my bed and shoots a mixture of water and Tylenol up my feeding tube and connects my IV to an antibiotic drip. My veins keep pushing out the IV, so each time the nurse arrives to give me a dose of antibiotics she has to thread the needle back into my skin. She's stained the inside of my arms purple.

The nurse tells my girlfriend she lived with a feeding tube for years. I take this common suffering and place it under my tongue like a smooth stone and hold it there. It makes it easier when she says I can't go home yet. In the mornings, she unwraps the gauze that covers the drain in my neck and evaluates the amount of discharge. The second drain, the one that isn't wrapped in gauze, empties into a clear plastic ball that is clipped to my hospital bed. I call it my blood grenade because it is filled with thin, bright liquid.

"Veel puss," she says, showing me a glob of yellow material produced from my throat.

"Okay," I say, my voice graveling and sore.

Before my first operation, they told me I might lose my voice.
The fistula in my throat snaked right by my vocal chords. The
chance of clipping a chord was high. After surgery, I writhed in
my post-surgery gurney, surfing the green wave of morphine. The
head of a beautiful man with wide pink eyes floated above my bed.
Stethoscope, dangle of curls, dimples. From his perch on the ceiling,
he smiled thick slabs of tooth.

"How are you feeling?" whispered the disembodied head.

I gave the beautiful head a thumbs up. Universal sign for perfect.
The head grinned again and injected my calf with a blood-hot
liquid.

I didn't attempt to talk for hours. I was terrified my voice would
be gone. When I finally opened my mouth, I was back in my shared
hospital room. A curtain hung between me and another woman.
I felt intrinsically connected to her. She would be breathing the
same air particles when I found out if I could still speak. I would be
skating through my opium daze when she got the worst news of her
entire life. I opened my mouth and a frightened noise appeared in
my ear. My voice. Still there.

"Hello," I said to myself. "Hello, hello."

Time is thick. I crawl through each minute on my knees. Instead
of sleeping, I scroll social media on my phone. I stop on a picture of Tonya standing next to a houseboat on the King Canal in
Amsterdam. She is gripping her hat as if the wind might flip it

off her head. Above her, seagulls slice the sky. I see pictures like this all the time: people I know walking along the cobbled roads, under scalloped roofs and seventeenth-century facades and beside houseboats moored to the side of city streets. But Tonya, she's not supposed to be here. She's supposed to be in Colorado posing next to life-changing Summer Body shakes she made as part of her ketogenic diet and updating her followers on her progress toward becoming a personal trainer.

Something sad skitters alongside Tonya's pictures. Maybe it's her absent husband, that droop-eyed, Ken-doll of a man I've never met. When I probe his Facebook, I find pictures of him posing with AK-47s in army fatigues, his bloodshot eyes boring into the lens. I find anti-Muslim explainer posts and memes of Barack Obama dressed up as an ape. The husband is military, serving overseas for his third time. Tonya's personal trainer posts are punctuated by updates on her husband's tour. There are pictures of her and her dog, who she refers to as her son. She does not smile with her eyes in these pictures. But she never has.

The woman I share a room with has cancer in her jaw. The doctor plans to remove part of the woman's hip bone in order to make her another jaw. My girlfriend reports this to me as she listens to the doctor explain the woman's prognosis on the other side of the curtain. I hear the woman crying in Dutch.

When we are alone in the room at night, noises come from the machines that have been inserted into our skin and tucked into our orifices. I hear the steady drip, drip of the feeding tube filling my stomach. I hear the woman next to me snore and groan. Her IV bag sizzles. Her moans are guttural. No translation necessary. They come digested, one animal to another.

I fart and burp because the feeding tube liquid burns my gut with its lactose formula. The stuff is probably packed with BPA and GMO and other acronyms I try to avoid. I take a selfie with my head on the pillow. God, it's pitiful. I text my mom the picture.

"Hi, Mom," I say in the text.

Robot emoji, robot emoji, robot emoji, robot emoji.

The feeding tube extends from my nose like a string of misplaced intestine and the drains drip from my neck. *Bionic person*, I think. Tubing going in and out. Non-human fluid mixing with human stuff. Human stuff draining out. *Robot man*.

"You look beautiful," my girlfriend's aunt told me when she saw me. She meant I looked skinny.

I Google feeding tube diet, and it actually exists. Models use it to regulate their caloric intake. They languish in bed for weeks, just like me, pumping nothing but liquid up their nose. When they emerge from their purge, they are thin as a sprig of clover.

I look out of my window. The square of world: my view for the last month. Pink dawn light. Cold outside, though I can't feel the air. The way the arms of the trees look from my window just tell me it's shivering. People who visit bring the smell of winter on their sweaters: leaf and sleet and tongues of coffee.

I am in a university hospital, so I see students most days. I scrutinize the sidewalk as if Tonya might be there because that's the age she's frozen in my mind no matter how many Summer Body photos she posts of her as a thirtyish woman. She's perpetually seventeen, always in soccer shorts and that lucky number 7 jersey sprinting down the field.

Next week, I will do a swallow test where I take a sip of something bright purple and poisonous-looking. An X-ray will capture the liquid dying my throat as I drink. I imagine the ink streaking my intestines full of radioactive fluid. If the liquid goes straight down and doesn't slip through a fistula, my surgery was successful. If the fistula is still there, I'll have to have another surgery. Each subsequent surgery gets more complicated. The scar tissue will be thicker, denser, and the chance of permanent damage to the area increases.

Once I leave the hospital, after my drains are removed and my stitches clipped, I will have a scar braided across my throat. Tonya has a scar, too. Hers runs along the spine. Scoliosis. During college, she would go into the bathroom stall to change out of her soccer jersey. She didn't undress in front of the team like the rest of us to reveal a sports bra and rolled up Umbro shorts cutting into her girl belly. She kept the spine scar hidden. She kept the body hidden. But I had seen it, thick keloid of a thing snaking from shoulder wing to sacrum, in my dorm room while candles burned inside paper lanterns.

My doctor, who looks like a literal angel, comes to my bed and tells me in perfect English that he has a positive feeling about the surgery but also that it took longer than he expected and that the scars were so bad from the previous infection that he could hardly see anything. I imagine his thick fingers holding tiny utensils that can repair tissue, vein, and chord. But I can't. The doctor, Van Stijn, reeks of cigarette smoke. He is younger than I am. A practical teenager and smelling of nicotine. His eyes are tired and alive. His hair is smeared in greasy curls just above his eyebrows. I'm reminded of an anecdote my girlfriend told me once about a brain surgeon friend who binged on cocaine and OxyContin and would spend entire weekends in the Hilton with a fleet of French escorts. The brain surgeon would perform surgeries completely hungover or high on speed.

It doesn't seem fair that Van Stijn has seen inside my throat; that he has fucked with my fifth chakra, the chakra that if fucked with can hinder creativity, create shyness, heighten anxiety, cause detachment and fear of speaking—and I know nothing whatsoever about him. All I know is that he smokes and has skin like poured cream. I want to know about his sex life. I wish, very sincerely, that he is gay. It seems important that he own a cock ring.

Van Stijn asks if I have any questions. I freeze. I have an immense amount of questions. My questions can fill the room. They can last all day. But I can't summon a single one.

"Not really," I say. "All good."

When I met Tonya, she was dating a hippie who was an active member of the Young Unitarian Universalists of Alabama. He made the best Irish soda bread I'd ever had. The only soda bread I'd ever had. He baked it in the off-campus house he lived in, a Georgian-style mansion with a sad paint job and a broad front porch that leaned to the left. He wore suspenders over his tie-dye. *A boy who bakes!* Tonya liked to say. Tonya and I were freshman. Both strikers on the college soccer team. A waiter asked us if we were sisters, which we loved, which made Tonya shriek. *Sisters!* Soon, sisters turned to twins. *Are you twins?* People would ask. We didn't look alike at all. The twinning was psychospiritual. Tonya was feline and loud. I was canine and quiet. I walked her to class, right to the door, because I didn't want to be apart a second longer than necessary. We swallowed each other's sentences, spoke in a garble of code words and pseudonyms that only we could decipher. I'd never wanted to be so close to another person. If I could find a zipper on her scoliosis scar and pull it down, step inside her skin and into the wet of her, I would have.

"Lesbians," I heard a teammate mutter.

The word twisted and burned in my ear. We bought matching puka shell necklaces. We filled a Nalgene with stolen granola from the school cafeteria and lived on the sugar-hardened buds for days. We discovered French press coffee and drank it by the liter until our chests pounded and our hands shook. We snorted cayenne pepper. *The fastest way to see God.* That's what Tonya told me. She believed in God. I began praying to impress her. I got on my knees and recited beautiful sonnets of prayer. I memorized Bible verses, wrote them on construction paper with smelly magic marker, and taped them over my desk. One day, my dormmate disappeared without a word and left all her stuff behind, even the 3-D velvet poster of a jaguar she had hung with care on our armoire. Tonya moved in. We slept in the same twin bed as if fulfilling the prophecy others had made about us. *Twins.* The top bunk. *Lesbians.* She kept saying how she was going to find me a hippie, too. She'd say this while she curled up against me, hot buttered breath in my ear.

When Van Stijn leaves, my nurse comes in and hooks me up to my antibiotic drip. She looks like Tonya. I notice it then and not a second earlier. After the drip is done, 25 minutes, the nurse says I can take a brief walk around the hospital as long as I drag my IV station next to me. I figure out how to loop my blood grenades through the IV rack securely. I'm terrified the grenade might fall and rip the drain out of my neck with the sheer force of gravity.

I shuffle through the halls of the hospital. The walls are painted a soft orange and art hangs on them. I stop in front of a mural of TLC. Lisa Lopes looks like a kind of saint of pain. I shuffle on. I walk out of the front door even, and no one stops me. There are a few patients outside in their smelly sweatpants and loose sweaters. The air stiffens me, but it feels so good to encounter anything other than the sterile machine-washed buzz of the hospital against my skin. I breathe until my lungs go raw. I'm so hungry. I want to chew anything, sip anything. My nose hurts, and I feel the tubing scratch against my tonsils. I told my girlfriend to ask the nurse about it.

"That's normal," the nurse said, sad-eyed with understanding.

Tonya's photos. A ferry ride to the film museum in North Amsterdam. A solemn selfie in front of Rembrandt's *The Night Watch* at the Rijksmuseum.

I could just say, "Hi, I see you're in Amsterdam."

I could ask what she is doing here, tell her I live here, too. We could get coffee in the hospital cafe. Or she could. I could continue extracting nutrients from my feeding tube drip while she drinks her latte. I could ask her how she got from dating a no-nukes Jesus-loving hippie in Birkenstocks to being married to a member of the NRA.

Tonya must know where I am. That I'm in Amsterdam. We don't have to tell anyone basic details anymore. Everyone just knows. The internet fills in the past. I imagine deleting all of my social media accounts and internet-disappearing for a year, then mailing postcards with updates to 10 chosen people. Tonya has seen me in my new pictures. Thin chin fuzz. Boyish slacks. Chest I've tried to flatten down with two sports bras. I wonder what she thinks of this new identity, the queerness I now wear on my body like a tuxedo or a second skin. Maybe this person was a secret I had been keeping from her.

It was our last night in Alabama before winter break. The spins or something worse. Cayenne up our noses. Stumbling home in the cold. Cold! Alabama could get so cold. The damp air teemed with winter. Tonya and I were singing a song by Hole, and her hippie was trailing us. His cowboy boots beat the ground like a heart. The sodium lights rounded the quad and the kudzu vines ascended the buildings. Or was it ivy. Something green and smothering. Before I knew it, the hippie was in front, and the three of us were running over the pavement toward the cemetery. We found a headstone and sat in front of it, above a buried body. Tonya and I looked at each other like *creepy*.

"This didn't use to be a cemetery," the hippie told us. "This used to be a home for orphan girls. Then one girl fell asleep with a cigarette in her fingers and BOOM."

The way he said boom lit a match in my mouth.

"The whole placed burned up, and a bunch of the girls died," said the hippie.

"Died," Tonya said.

I could tell she wanted to be awed by this story so the hippie could feel like he had said something interesting.

So many dead girls, I thought. The faces of tombstones stared at me white as ghosts. I could almost make out lips, mouths, girl nose, eroded into the marble.

Who was this girl before she died? The one whose grave grew the clovers on which we sat? I looked to Tonya, and she was looking at her hippie. I'd seen that expression before in other girls, parted mouth, delicate raise of one eyebrow, when they gazed at their boyfriends. Adoration. Or something. I'd seen that expression in the way she looked at me, too. I willed it out of her, her desire. In my mind, I said: *Look at me like I'm your boyfriend*. And she did.

I hobble to the elevator. It opens, and a mother and child catch me in their plate-sized eyes. My throat gauze sags with pink soggy stuff, and I'm clenching my blood grenade in my fist.

"Sorry," I gravel.

"It's okay!" The mother practically screams.

I see a pleading in her eyes, but I don't know how to help her. The elevator shoots up. I stand, wide-legged in the middle of it, hunched over in exhaustion.

Back in my room, I sleep the feverish sleep of someone on medical grade paracetamol and vitamin-enriched nose sludge. I thrash and toss in my bed. My roommate is in surgery, so it's only my machine that's making noise. I wake up when they wheel the woman back in. She's moaning a kind of boozy nonsense. Throughout the afternoon she starts to vomit blood. I push the button near my bed that's shaped like a stick figure wearing a dress. It means: *Nurse!*

A nurse runs in and wheels her out quickly.

"Hi," I write to Tonya through an Instagram DM.

Five minutes later, under my message, is the word: Seen.

Hey," she writes back. First words exchanged in years. Normal enough.

Where is she? A brown bar on the Herengracht? A coffee shop in the Jordaan? I don't ask.

The hippie passed out against the headstone with his pants undone, his dick in his fist. Ostensibly a threesome was supposed to happen, but he drank too much moonshine. At first, we were afraid he died or went blind because when you drink moonshine that can happen. Then he started to snore, and we knew it was okay. Tonya started telling me made-up stories about the dead orphan girls who burned up in the fire. Then her stories were over, and it was just the two of us without a man to normalize our desire.

The rest of the night I can't remember. Or won't remember. Maybe that's the same thing. Wet and tongue-y. I told her *please don't* when she tried to touch my chest. I already knew I didn't want my breasts to be touched like that, like they were just a part of some girl. Unzipped jeans. Sweet flower underwear. I stared at the hippie slouched and unconscious on the burial mound, soft dick gripped like a useless weapon in his large hand. Head fallen to the side, mouth gaping, eyes shut. An off-duty guard. Useless. Tonya's hot hands against my cold skin. I wince at the memory because I could tell, even then, that she was making up those noises. Those noises weren't real. She manufactured them just for me, in that moment, but I still can't figure out why. She rolled on top of me and humped my leg. I held my breath until she stopped, and it was over.

Van Stijn comes into my room. Time to swallow test. He rolls me to the radiation room. No one puts one of those anti-radiation blankets over my womb or chest. They just have me chug a glass of bitter liquid, the first sip I've taken in a month, and stand behind a machine. They say: *Klaar.* That sounds a lot like Claire, which is what most people call me.

The woman with the cancer in her jaw is still gone when they roll me back in. I wonder where they took her. Beautiful yellow tulips appeared on her nightstand while we were gone. I wait for my results. The nurse comes in and gives me a shot that will keep my blood from clotting. Every time I see her I want to call her Tonya. Maybe Tonya is moving to Europe. Maybe her military husband will be stationed at the Campbell Barracks Army Base in Heidelberg, and they will live in Germany together, and Tonya will open her own CrossFit box. Maybe she will have a baby and bring the baby to see me and say, *This is your Uncle Claire.*

I check my Instagram. Tonya hasn't written anything after her *Hey.* She's the gregarious one, the one who always knew what to say. Maybe she's afraid that her humping my leg all those years ago turned me gay, that if she sees me, she'll have to confront it.

Van Stijn. Here he is. His face is solemn. He claps his hands and rubs them together like he's got a plan.

He says, "We're going to have to do this all over again."

The nurse lets me go for a walk again.

"Just please don't smoke," she says.

Her English is perfect this time. I wonder if she had been lying to me. I wonder if she memorized that one sentence. I drag my IV station past the picture of Saint Lisa and head to the cafeteria so I can watch people eat cheese sandwiches. The words *do this over again* wreck against each other in my mind. My gaze smolders on a man as he heads to a table with a sack of bread swinging at his hip. I imagined myself sitting down at a table and just stuffing food into my mouth until globs of chewed bread come out into my drain. *Fix that, Van Stijn.* Then, I see her. She passes by the hospital doors outside. Same long braid I've seen on Instagram. Same pink jacket. American mountain fleece. *Tonya.* Did she somehow know I was here? Was she coming to look for me? Maybe she went up to my room and found me gone.

I hobble toward the door. It slides open. A hard gray sky swirls above me and snow falls across the ugly compound. Tonya is walking quickly toward the sidewalk, taking the stairs two at a time, her head pointed away from the falling snow.

"Tonya," I say, but my voice comes out in a croak, strangled.

I drag my IV stand behind me until I reach the stairs. I'm not sure how to get down them. I lean against the railing, call her name again. I tuck my blood grenade into my armpit so it won't fall and start my slow descent. Tonya is almost to the street now. It looks like she has headphones in. Otherwise, she would hear me. She really would.

"Sir!"

I hear a man rush up behind me.

"Oh," he says, because now that he sees me he's not sure what I am. "Are you okay? I can't let you leave like this."

He's a nurse, but he looks so much like Tonya's hippie. The hippie-look-alike lifts me up, and I almost drop my blood grenade.

"I know her," I whisper. "Call her name. Say, *Tonya*."

God bless him, the man does it. He screams Tonya. His voice is so loud. It is a booming man voice, and it commands the listening. Tonya turns. My chest falls. It feels like a hand is squeezing me. The hippie's hands are squeezing me.

"Oh," I say, staring into the woman's freckled face. It's not Tonya. Her forehead is too tall. Her chin is an odd geometry. It isn't Tonya. There's been a mistake, but I still lift my hand. The blood grenade is clutched in the hand I lift. I wave it back and forth. The blood sloshes in its clear plastic ball.

"Hi, Tonya," I say anyway.

Dance!

Connie did not like to leave the tall canal house on the Prinsengracht where she lived with her pink dolphin, Blondie. She didn't go out unless it was to the marine research center, where she worked night shifts as a custodian, mopping the floors with warm suds as the blue light of the aquariums held her. When Connie walked over to Blondie's tank in her living room, the water a flushed rose, she pressed her palm against the glass. It felt alive. She imagined her body mazed-through with glass tubes that pumped roses and dolphins. Her body might as well be made of things she could see. Flowers and water and glass. She pushed play. A recording of her own voice, half-speaking and half-singing, began.

Connie cycled through the tourist-thronged streets toward the only pet store in town that sold dolphin food. On the streets: so many people. People walked with woolen coats pulled tight at the collar, hats tipped down against the mean, wet spray. People biked with umbrellas held above them, used just one hand to steer. She hated to be so close to people, these dirty people with their cell phones and their headache-inducing perfumes and their capitalist caw. Pollution frothed in puddles. Rain yelled at the ground. Cyclists veered off the road to find dryness inside shops. Connie rode past a group of people huddled together beneath a bridge but refused to join those ringing out their pants and jackets. She kept going, relieved to be the only one outside, making her way through the Vondelpark as the rain beat down and the wind knocked leaves from the trees and scattered trash through the streets.

Inside, the pet food store smelled like feces and urine and calcified mice. Mold grew in furry patches on the walls. The ceiling sagged like a wet diaper. A teenage store clerk with a greasy ponytail approached Connie, but she drew her jacket across her face and said, "I need no help!"

Something about the clerk's mouth reminded Connie of Sven, the woman from Iceland who had once lived as an anti-squatter next door. Maybe it was the way the clerk smiled, so coy, as if he knew her—which of course, he did. Everyone knew Connie or at least could identify her by sight. The knowing smile. Uh, huh. Sven had smiled that way, too. Sven had smiled like she knew Connie— not-yet-famous, perfectly square, pre–dolphin song Connie.

Connie used to pass Sven on their stoop in the red-streaked dawn when she was coming home from work and Sven was departing to go to it. By day, Sven made her living as a sex worker. By night, she took classes in computer programming, learned 1s and 0s, Python, and Objective C. Sven's window was jammed into a lesser trafficked area of the Red Light District, down an alley paved with crude cobbles that also housed Connie's favorite bakery. Sven would sit on a stool with the curtains drawn open, her pinched face pulling eye contact from strangers.

One day, Connie had stopped in front of Sven's window and raised a hand. She lifted up the bag of hot bread like *want some?* Sven waved back, and the rest happened very naturally. Sven was the first woman Connie ever loved. She visited during the weekend, and they would drink cups of hot water and eat salted herring and spread their coats down like blankets in front of Blondie's tank. The pink light slipped across their bodies.

Before the fame had quarantined Connie to a hermetic life, she would go with Sven to patronize the anarchist house on the Spuistraat where Sven's friends performed guerrilla theater and housed bedroom parties and screened documentaries about prison abolitionism in Russia. They ate vegan popcorn from plastic bowls and sat on a floor so unwashed it had sprouted a kind of hair. The graffiti on the walls fumed around them, caked in decades of sweat and breath. Sven rubbed at the knots in her neck. Connie felt like she had stumbled into a warm womb.

Now Connie found her way to the back of the pet store where crates of water held marine animals of all kinds. She stood before a captive dolphin, a manta ray, a baby shark. The tanks in the pet store made Connie's brain feel like a forgotten galaxy of muck. She would never buy an animal here, even though they probably needed her the most. Their auras were contagious, cancerous, cadmium-colored.

Connie watched the shark's nose pump against the glass because the tank was too small to hold him. She gave him a name: Prince of the Caged.

During her long nights cleaning the halls of the marine research center, Connie found herself doing a little research of her own. One evening, two scientists had emerged from their laboratory dens. Their excitement was smelly. It transformed into brown moons that stained the fabric under their armpits. Their faces looked like crotch mushrooms. They paused in the doorway of an office, elated. Their bodies squirmed with success. They did not even lower their voices. Connie mopped in their direction. These men, white beards and white coats and white faces, conducted research in the field of Animal Translation Studies. *Access*, thought Connie, swallowing down a wad she'd wished to spit. The scientists had, that very day, successfully spoken to a dolphin. And the dolphin had spoken back. They had broken through.

Not fair, thought Connie.

In the lead scientist's office, with only the light of his desk lamps to guide her, Connie discovered a digital library of phonemes. The scientists had attached recordings of dolphin pulses, snaps, and whistles to actual human words. Here were common greetings, condolences, expressions of obvious anger.

Connie began to teach herself the language. She stole thumb drives filled with entire dictionaries of sound. She put her face to her computer screen until her eyes dried out and listened to dolphin prattle until her ears murmured. She whistled and hummed

and cawed at Blondie until one day she could tell from the way he
whirled with enthusiasm through his water that he understood her.

Connie wrote a song in dolphin and played it while she went
to the research center so Blondie wouldn't be lonely. The song was
a mix of Connie's voice and actual musical melodies. Melodies, not
tones! In between the melodies she spoke facts about humans so
that Blondie could learn about her. For instance, she instructed,
humans must put their feces in a toilet. Humans in Amsterdam eat
mostly sandwiches of cheese. Holland is located in the upper west
corner of a continent called Europe. She showed the song to Sven,
and they danced through the descants as if it were another time and
Drone Wave had not yet come. Sven twirled Connie through the
living room and Blondie seemed to dance with them. Outside, the
lazy water in the canals seemed to dance, too.

For as many years as Connie could remember, the most popular
music in the world had been a single note played for minutes at a
time called Drone Wave. The single note played in cafes, hummed
into earbuds, rung out in the grand open spaces of Central Station.
People no longer danced. Instead of dancing, people stood in the
sound with their eyes closed. They raised their hands above their
heads and spun in a slow circle. Not dancing, but trembling. Connie
despised Drone Wave. She longed for music from another time:
Whitney Houston, Beyoncé, something heavy metal. Connie's
favorite music had words, multiple notes, and even, sometimes, a
melody. Oh, that feeling, like her face was melting, when a song
hit a chorus that she loved. Drone Wave could never do that to the
chest.

Connie had composed only this one song for Blondie, just this single one. But she had made the mistake of playing her song at high volumes in her apartment. The notes kicked her walls. Sound scattered across the street and struck people. It drew the masses toward her door. People gathered outside her steps. They held parties in the streets in front of her house. They danced in mesh tops and put glow sticks in their mouths and wore underwear of faux fur. It had been enough to slide the country out of the trance of Drone Wave and into a new sensation of sound people named Animal Podcast-Punk. That was all it took to ruin her life. Nothing had been the same after that.

Though Connie had been well paid by the record company that bought the rights to her song, she'd kept her custodial job. She needed the ritual. The monotonous tasks jiggled her heart. It felt religious, or at least ceremonial, to walk up and down the vacant halls of the marine center and bow before the dorsal fins, the blistered bodies of man-of-war, and cephalopod tentacles stippled with suction cups. She knocked on the manta ray tank and stared into the pinhole of its eye. Its cape rippled in the water.

The building was unpeopled and silent but for the calm whir of the heating system that buzzed and coughed. Glass held the water back. *Like Moses,* Connie thought, as she walked through the halls where water could rush. *Let my people go.* The pure, clean glass glinted like a villain's teeth. Even with so much water around her, the air inside the halls felt surgical, rinsed of any condensation. Her mouth parched. Connie's skin peeled and her lips chapped.

She leaned against the mop until the grit and grime and gum stains disappeared under her. The laminate shined.

Connie would never give up this job. She commuted home from work just before dawn when no one was out except cruisers and clumps of coked-out kids. She cycled under a raw pre-dawn sky, fresh and star-specked. The commute was the only time she left her house and she knew she needed it, these pilgrimages across town. Outside her door, no one congregated any longer. She made sure her house was silent as a museum. There would be nothing for anyone to listen to.

Connie couldn't leave her apartment without at least one person saying, "Aren't you that *gal* with the Dolphin Song?" Connie hated the word gal as much as she hated questions and strangers. So she had everything she needed delivered through Amazon Prime: groceries, 101 documentaries on meditation, dental floss. Normally she even arranged to pick up dolphin food from the marine research center so she didn't have to go to pet stores, but this week, she had forgotten the cans of food by its door. *Drat*, she had thought, peering through the plywood she had hammered over her windows. A slit of light blinked through. It was a special kind of food made out of raw, wild-caught sea turtle and squid, unfindable on Amazon.

Now, as she stood in line at the pet store, Connie's song began to play. It poured like syrup from the speakers. It covered everyone in goo, and they got high. It lit the air. Connie stood in line and listened to the hoots and whistles and clicks her tongue had recorded in her bedroom, the synthetic beats she had strung together on the piano inside her laptop. The men and women in the store started to dance. Dance! It embarrassed her, the way they flung their stiff bodies through the pet store and flailed their limbs. Dancing in public, as much as she had once wanted it, now made her uncomfortable. To see people lose their inhibition like that? It should be a private thing. In her brain, Connie hummed a single note, Drone Wave-ish, and felt her tense neck release.

She told herself: *This is just an overactive third-eye chakra. You're being paranoid.*

She told herself: *No one recognizes you here. They can't tell who you are because your beanie is pulled down over your face. Even if they notice you, they are being polite and will let you go about your day.*

But here came a woman toward her, one eye wild with suspicion.

"Here she is here she is here she is," said the woman, a gnarled finger outstretched into a hook. "Here she is here she is here she is."

Connie clutched the dolphin food to her chest. Even with her beanie pulled across her eyes, they knew her. A headache moved into her neck—*Sven, why wasn't Sven here?* Connie had once been able to leave her house without a soul looking her way. She'd faded into the crowd of black coats. Now, this. Always, this. She peered through a hole in the pilled fabric of her beanie. Connie could smell herself. A fishy odor squirmed up and out of her turtleneck. She had rubbed a deodorant crystal furiously against her pits this morning, but it did nothing. She had scraped her tongue and stimulated her lymphatic system with Ayurvedic skin brushing, circular strokes on the stomach to relieve digestion, but still, her body rebelled. It leaked a stench. A necklace of acne had recently appeared on her chest and a red fear rash on her face. She worried she would become sick all alone inside that house. Better sick and alone, she thought, than bombarded like this.

People became a mob and the mob circled her, gnashed their teeth and lashed their arms as if to say, *Dance! Dance! Dance!* They wanted a concert! Another song! *Dance, Connie, dance!*

Connie dropped the cans of dolphin food and ran into the rain.

She wished Sven was with her now, that Sven could have gone out to get dolphin food instead. She would have. Sven would have done that. Sven with her pink lipstick marks on cups and her head filled with 1s and 0s. Sven who could tie a cherry stem with her tongue and pick Connie up with strong arms and a deep laugh, spin her in her arms. With Sven, Connie's third-eye chakra did not over-activate. Sven was like a black tourmaline stone, calm and pure and pinning her back to the ground. But Sven now sat in some open office layout in the orange sun of Silicon Valley, typing the future into a screen. What would Sven do, if she were there? Sven would tell Connie to waltz. Just dance with the people! Give them what they want. Play your song. Make a concert. Touch the lovestuff.

A handless girl now sat on Sven's stool in that alley tinted with appeltaart and sugar. Once, Connie had raised a bag of hot bread to the new girl. Nothing. Not even a look. Sven said Connie should come visit her in California, of course she should, but they both knew it would never happen. Connie could never get on a plane. Never leave Blondie. Never sit on a chemtrail as it streaked through the sky.

Bad
Dangerous

The yogurt in our fridge reminds me of sperm. Clyde the Dane's sperm to be exact. His creamy baby makers, those swimmers he will give us again tonight. I grab the coffee can and light the stove. In the other room, Frankie sleeps and does not ovulate. My body is the one that's doing that.

Frankie and I made a list of all the traits we wanted in a donor. Gentle, meek of spirit, witty, no intravenous drug use, not right wing, spiritual but non-religious, nurtures an artistic skill, good relationship with mother. Creative is on our list, too. And Clyde the Dane works as a Creative. That's his actual job title. He helps tech companies convince people to share human-identifying information like voice IDs, face structure, fingerprints, geo-locations, photo libraries, home addresses, and retina maps in exchange for cool stuff like being able to ask a robot if you can have groceries delivered to your door by 5 p.m. that very evening.

Clyde the Dane is shepherding us toward the future. Me and Frankie specifically, but also the entire world. In addition to those creative skills, Clyde the Dane is dewy with youth. His skin is phero-mone-rich and smells like softness. Young and virile. Clyde the Dane with his tender eyes and lips that bulge open just a touch, of course he wants to help us. He wants to help everyone. He wants to help the whole world.

Frankie doesn't even let us have smartphones.

"Maybe his sperm is radioactive," she once said. "From all that computer work."

"Maybe that means we'll have superhero babies."

"Maybe that means we're just shooting thick milk."

In my dreams, I kayak through a sea of Danish sperm. Waves crash in the distance and I am on a boat alone, rowing toward an island filled with babies that need me.

A Dutch ballerina recently moved into the apartment above us, and it was like she brought elephants. Herds. The word ballerina had sounded so delicate, poised. I imagined someone floating just above the floor, landing on it only long enough to make contact with the tips of her toes. I thought: thin, pin of a person with a mind sharp-ened to a point and rituals that send her early to bed. Every day and night after the ballerina moved in, it felt like she was pulling the planks from the floor above us, sloughing off the wall skin, conduct-ing surgery on the bowels of her kitchen.

"Ballerinas can be very aggressive," said Frankie.

This month's ovulation corresponds with the new moon. It seems like I should perform some ritual, like paint the walls with stolen menstrual blood or bang hammers onto metal planks at dawn like my friend Pigeon does with his witch friends.

"Let's just get Clyde out of here ASAP, and I'll inseminate you," Frankie had said, raising an eyebrow toward her hairline. "I think that's enough."

But that's not enough for Frankie. Not really. To prepare, she will make us light aromatherapy candles. We will sip kombucha from wine glasses for probiotic health. We will place jade, moonstone, and rose quartz on my body's acupressure points.

"The stones help your womb get ready to catch the sperm," Frankie said the first time.

"How?" I asked. "Do they send vibes down there and tell my womb to like redecorate or something? Make it nice for the sperm dudes so they'll stick around?"

"I don't know exactly," said Frankie. "But there's a goddess connection."

Once, Frankie and I ran into the ballerina on the stairs. I had already become obsessed with her heavy footfalls, the relentless crash bang through the night, and found myself putting an ear to the door as she passed by outside clompclompclomping up to her apartment.

"Hi, girls," said the ballerina when she saw us. She wore all black and not like a goth.

Girls.

The ballerina made a smiling motion by baring two rows of small yellow teeth. I bared my teeth back. She clutched a leopard print bag in her hands.

"Girls," she said again as if we needed an extra reminder of our gender. "I'm having some ballerinas from Mongolia over next week. They're going to stay with me while they rehearse for a show. It'll be five of us total, so we might be extra loud. Just a couple months."

"Okay," said Frankie. "No biggie."

No biggie? I mouth this to Frankie because I'm noise-phobic so it was a biggie and partially because she never says *No biggie*. Who does?

"Five ballerinas from Mongolia," I said to Frankie when we were on the street alone, walking to the corner store for *bruisend* water, which means sparkling water, which I've never stopped thinking of as bruised. Bruised water.

I felt panicky. I couldn't help it.

"It's none of our business," said Frankie. "Who she has over."

"I can't conceive a child while I listen to five dancers from Mongolia clomp above me!"

I drink my coffee while Frankie sleeps and Google *How do lesbians shoot sperm?* I've read these blogs countless times, but I keep coming back to Google like an addict, itching for the same information over and over again. I find an advertisement for a dildo that ejaculates "just for lesbians." It's called The Spermette, which sounds to me like some kind of kinky kitchen toy. I eye the photograph of a dyke daddy with spiky hair gazing at me from the website. I slam the laptop shut and gnaw at my thumb. Frankie's going to make us do organismic meditation before we use Clyde's semen. I just know it. She always wants to OM when she's thinks I've been distant, and I've been a practical mutant for weeks, disappearing in the morning and staying at the pub all night until only the canal rats are left on the streets, and I'm sauntering home alone like a young James Dean in my vegan leather jacket. I've been drinking Club Mates, nothing alcoholic, but just being near drunk people and witnessing their bad decisions makes me feel dangerous and alive. Last night I sipped my Club Matte in the pub and talked to Butch behind the bar. Butch's mustache looked dapper with her new glorious afro. I told her so. I told Butch how Frankie and I were going to have a baby. She loved the idea. Slapped the bar. Said she would crochet a onesie for us. Said we could have a baby shower right there.

I'm getting stress sweats and craving cigarettes and weed. The coffee has done nothing except make me want to do jumping jacks. It's already the afternoon! The sun broods all orange and full in the white sky and rains heat down on the city. I hit the town in a sleeveless tee, sniff my pit hair to make sure I don't smell like funk. Today, I think, might be my last day as a true daddy-less bachelor, empty-wombed and angular.

I stop by the fish cart to get a herring broodje with extra pickles. Sometimes when I eat fish, everything feels better. The chewing sends happiness through me like hot steam. Wait, I think, I've heard something about fish and pregnancy. *Bad. Dangerous.*

Whatever, says my brain, which sounds a lot like Frankie. Just eat the herring.

The park is filled with tourists lobbing Frisbees, joints dangling from their mouths. Bad Euro-techno and American pop blares from personal wireless devices. A group of French men try to ride bicycles but keep half-falling or getting cut off by Dutch people. I watch to see if they're going to eat shit and ruin those nice tailored trousers. The Mongolian ballerinas haven't moved in yet, but I keep imagining the parade of dancers running up the stairs just as we're getting the sperm ready. Everything is always about to be ruined.

The girl working the fish cart is cute as hell. She keeps plowing her hand through the fish bins and pulling out fists of scaled bodies. They look muscular and tough even when they're dead. The girl doesn't flinch as she digs into the bins. Blood is smeared all over her apron. She stares at me with no emotion behind her eyes, which is a common Dutch thing to do, and asks in English if she can help me. It's always an insult when someone doesn't think I'm Dutch. What is it this time? Probably the baseball cap or maybe the grin plastered across my face. It screams American.

Sometimes, like right now, I realize I'm wearing a flat bill cap and get self-conscious. I catch a glimmer of myself in a window as I pass it or see an expression reflected in the face of a stranger, like fish girl here, and I realize I don't look how I want to look. Sometimes putting on boy clothes does not make me feel more like a boy, but more like a girl, as if the hipless long coats or flat-chested shirts draw attention to all the things I'm not instead of infusing me with a kind of androgynous serum.

I have a friend in Seattle, an old-school, suit-wearing butch. Her cargo pants and workman shirts fit like a second skin. After she got married, her wife couldn't conceive a child, so my friend decided to step in and try. She got pregnant on the first go. I thought it was sort of like nature saying *fuck you. You do have a womb under those boxer shorts and Dickies.* During her pregnancy, she went through a total transformation. She began to wear dresses and grew out her hair. She's now a different person on the outside. Soft or something. I don't know.

I try to be inspired by this, like, we can recreate ourselves endlessly. But my brain snags. I check myself out in the plexiglass siding of the fish cart while I eat my fish sandwich and contemplate how I would feel if pregnancy made me want to wear a dress. That's when I see them behind me: Clyde the Dane and the ballerina sitting on a park bench. *Flirting.*

Frankie knows I get obsessed with people. I'm a Cancer after all. I reach out my crab claw and snap someone in my pinchers and won't let go. It's compulsive. I just keep pinching the shit out of this new thing until one day I lose interest and let it go.

Once the ballerina came to our door, knocked, and asked me to show her how to use her thermostat. I felt like a mechanic or something.

"Uh. Sure. Let me see here. I think it works like this."

I jammed my finger into some buttons. Mine and Frankie's thermostat had been dead for years. We just wear thick sweaters and two pairs of wool socks when it gets cold. Frankie would think it was hilarious, me fixing anything, but I was overcome with a new dedication to understand the ballerina's thermostat. It was a test of some kind.

Just how resourceful are the dykes downstairs?

She would definitely call us lesbians. Not queers. *Girls.* Something very gender specific and impersonal sounding. Funny how that works.

I could feel the ballerina staring at me as I gazed at her thermostat in faux concentration. She dragged her eyes over my flannel and down to my Docs. I had already noticed that she wore ankle boots, the culprit I realized for the clomping. She, unlike Frankie and me, did not take her shoes off when she came inside. She stomped around in those booty heels. She had all of her pots and pans pulled out of the cupboard and spread across the floor. I gestured to them, said, "Some kind of art project?"

Her face looked fraught.

"Mice!" She said. "Mice! Do you have mice? I found mice droppings in my pots and pans and wanted to see if there was a rodent hole back there."

We did have mice, but I felt like I shouldn't admit it. I wanted her to imagine me as an immaculate mechanic, able to patch up mice holes, keep a kitchen clean, fix a heater with a turn of the screw.

I walk over to Clyde and the ballerina. Clyde's hair is twirled back into a messy man bun. His rumpled pants and striped shirt are exactly how I'd dress my baby, his non-son.

Clyde's smooth, office hands rest on his thighs. The ballerina sits upright, poised; some might say regal. A dollop of mayo from her fish sandwich has affixed itself to her lip crease. I tell her so, and she seems grateful. It appears as though Clyde and the ballerina are on a date. *Tinder*, I think. Fuming. Already I've gone there in my head. I've imagined Clyde coming to our apartment and ejaculating into a sterilized glass jar like he's done many times. Then I've imagined him going upstairs and copulating above us with the ballerina while we use his sperm one floor down. What if we both got pregnant with Clyde's babies at once? There would be two floors of Clydes. What if he has an orgy with the Mongolians and there are dozens of Clyde babies? Men can just do that, make entire baby armies.

Frankie and I told Clyde we'd let him know when we got pregnant. He eyes my midriff, flat as a board. He's wondering maybe if tonight the magic will happen.

Clyde seems amused when I tell him Frankie and I are neighbors with the ballerina.

"Convenient!" he says.

"When do your Mongolian visitors arrive?" I ask the ballerina, pretending like I am just now remembering it.

She looks confused. Everything about her is suspicious.

"Oh," she says. "They're not. That was canceled."

My grandfather once told me most of the things we spend time worrying about never happen. He's right again. But now in place of that worry, there's this one.

Clyde goes, "I was just talking about this new device I'm working on that lets you change songs on your Song-ify account by simply blinking your eyes. You have to wear these contact lens, but they're going to be so light you won't even be able to tell they're in your eyes at all. They'll be, like, a part of you. Like a remote control you actually control."

"Super nice!" says Clyde, as if to himself. He blinks quickly to demonstrate how he'd change songs.

"I can't wait to see what I'd look like as a baby," Clyde told me after he'd signed the legal document releasing his sperm to us. This was months ago. We had gone out for lunch and were eating the Dutch version of vegetarian tacos: flour tortillas with butter lettuce, tomatoes, sour cream, and Gouda cheese.

"I hope we have a boy," he had said.

We. I had to remind him *we* weren't having anything.

I used to really like Clyde. Maybe I even had a crush on him. I don't know. I used to get crushes on men all the time, but I never actually wanted to touch them. It's like my friend Ezra, who wanted to know what it would be like to go on a date with a woman, but he only thought about it sometimes and it was more like a science experiment and the woman would have to know he was only curious before the date so she didn't get the wrong idea. A puff of heteronormative firecrackery that he could bask in for a splendiferous moment. Then he could go back to normal life.

"I want to see myself in another person," Clyde had clarified. "See what I'd look like if my genes mixed with someone. With you!"

Something about that creeped me out. Was Clyde flirting?

We reached for the hot sauce at the same time, and our fingers touched.

Though, if I'm honest, I really did understand what he meant. But after that, any semblance of a crush disappeared. Poof. *Gone.*

On the way home, I imagine stopping by the fish cart and fucking the fish girl on the floor of the cart, right on top of all of those fish guts and blood smears. There's nothing I want more at this moment than to do that.

My friend Jo's girlfriend got pregnant, and now he wears a daddy breastfeeding bra called Milk Dudes over his chest scars so he can bond with his son. He carries the boy around in a Mei Tai and still goes to get flat whites from the street cart. It feels like the future. My future.

When I was young, I never imagined the future. The future always seemed like the credits at the end of the movie, something that was coming that I didn't look forward to or even want to watch. But now the future seems like it's here. Credits about to roll. Once I have a baby, the future will be my life. Babies are like little balls of future you have to keep from dying and shower with endless love. I imagine wearing a Milk Dude over my sports bra and staring at a little rosebud of a mouth. I imagine love for a human who doesn't exist yet filling my body with a soft orange light like the British voice on my meditation tapes instructs me to do.

What would it be like, to feel content with all of that?

Adorno

The van smells like muscles and open wounds. The merry-band of radicals who picked me up have two dozen water bottles filled with menstrual blood in the back ready for their direct action. Some of it, they tell me, was donated by friends before they left home. The stench is like deep water, covering us with its saline hand, forcing us to roll the windows down. Mo bleeds while she drives. It makes her seem noble, like her very body is participating in something great.

The Spanish landscape is unremarkable, just a stretch of highway weaving its way through tanned, weather-beaten hills around us. We've left behind the water and the mountains that quivered with life. I can still feel the ocean, even though it's nowhere to be seen; it pulls me like a tide, whispering: *come back.*

Rat hangs his head out of the passenger window, a dog with its tongue out and howling. He leans toward Mo and says, "Baby I can't wait to see the face of some fur-clad delegate wearing your blood."

"I'm fixing to pour it all over anyone I see wearing boots of stolen skin," Mo says. Her flat voice lacks the crescendo of emotion that clings to Rat's every utterance. "Then I'll purr in their face like a house cat."

I can't explain how lucky I feel to have lost my favorite leather jacket at that punk bar in Madrid. I always thought as long as leather was second-hand, it was okay to wear, but these guys are hardcore. They make a point of pooping outside in the grass as part of the African proverb they've etched in crude letters onto the van's dashboard: *Poop in the fields of the man who feeds you.* Part of life's circle, they say. They've strained the period blood of its clots so they can hide the clumps in the frozen meat section of grocery stores.

"So, what are your plans in Brussels, exactly?" I ask. "Like what's the direct action?"

"It's a secret, darling," Rat says, "but I'm going to put my trust in you because your energy field is sparkling like a diamond."

"Thanks," I say, feeling drawn in by the compliment.

"The EU Parliament is discussing a measure to make it mandatory that rabbits be moved from small battery cages to something just barely decent. Still awful. But a step in the right direction. Rabbits need better cages. Hell. Rabbits need no cages. We're there to advocate for them."

"People overlook the rabbits," says Dirk, who sits next to me in the back. "It's always chickens and cows and pigs in the spotlight. People forget about the exploitation of rabbits."

Rat nods in vigorous agreement.

"It's going down outside the European Parliament's metro stop. We're going to dress in rabbit costumes and go in the middle of the night and set up our blood bomb that will explode promptly at 7:30 the next a.m. Then WOOSH all over those expensive clothes they're wearing. Those dapper ass booty-boots."

"Your blood bomb?" I ask.

Mo eyes me in the rearview mirror. She reminds me of images I've seen of German children during the war, desperate eyes, stoic mouth, and a pale face destined for photographs. She grimaces under her buzz cut, or maybe it's her attempt at a smile. She doesn't trust me. Her eyes flit back to the road. Someone named Krenshaw sleeps in the seat behind Dirk, but they haven't stirred since I got into the van. They mutter something now, some dream language.

"You got it," says Rat. "That's a bomb filled with biomaterial from our biobank. We're talking plasma, teeth, nails, talons, fish scales, pieces of horse placenta, by-products of surgeries, animal embryos, human hair, dead house pets, roadkill. It's all going to rain down on the delegates going bright and early to their comfy little power jobs."

"It's going to raise attention for our biobank co-op, too," says Dirk.

Rat explains how they've rented a storage container in Barcelona and installed refrigerators where they keep the biomaterial. They use it themselves or donate the biomaterial to other vegan activists.

"First rule for the biobank," says Rat.

He bites into a raw, nut-butter sandwich. I'm not sure how he can eat with the putrid blood smell that's baking into us, but he chomps away.

"First rule is you cannot kill anything to get the material. It has to have died from natural causes or be found in nature or be stolen from fuckwads. No murdering yourself or buying. We found out someone tried to donate a bird brain they bought from a petrol station in Germany. Hell to the no. That's playing into the system 100%. That just puts money in their pockets."

"Yeah, well, Mick was a tool," says Dirk. "So, it was expected. He never got what this was really about."

"T to the OOL," says Rat.

"How do you get the stuff anyway?" I ask. "Like the teeth and stuff."

Now that I know it's more than menstrual blood I'm smelling but also placenta and questionably extracted surgical by-products, I feel sickness spilling up my esophagus. I follow Rat's lead and reach my head out of the window for fresh air. The wind pummels me.

"Well," Rat screams over the rush of wind. "Dirk over here is a dentist's assistant so he gets us human teeth real easy and Krenshaw works on a farm, so she can steal plenty of animal placentas and sometimes chunks of thigh or brain that the murderers are trying to discard in slop buckets."

I joined the We R Animals vegan bus outside of Barcelona. I ran into them mid-mindfulness walk around the grounds of a Benedictine monastery, repenting, self-flagellating with the soft vine of a tree, and fasting on fruit. I have to admit that part of the fast was a knee-jerk response to a weeklong cheese binge in France, but I decided to corral it into the more comprehensive punishment I was inflicting on myself. After all, I ruined someone's life.

I gazed up at one of many stone massifs that flanked the monastery. It looked like an eagle. *Fierce eagle*, I thought. *Your wings are stone, and you cannot fly.* The sky was the perfect pearl blue of the Mediterranean. *There are worse places to be flightless, fierce eagle,* I told the stone bird with my mind.

Over time, the wind had eroded the mountains here into penile shapes, schlong-like and bulbous. I hiked under the stone penises. Their rocky skin shifted between bruised pink and squeezed tangerine depending on the light. Info signs described the formations as needle-shaped, but I think they're prude. They're monks after all, so I couldn't blame them. I walked, brisk and delirious from hunger, through the phallic mountain range, stopping at each vista to pantomime shock at the beauty that rolled into the blue, smog-tipped range in the distance.

That's when I saw Rat, skinny and homeless looking and wearing nothing but a speedo. He was taking in the glorious views, leaning against a tree and making a scene of the way the sun smacked him in the face with her hot orange breath.

"Vitamins, man! Vitamins. The sun has so many vitamins!"

Rat turned toward me all nodding innocence and a little smug-mouthed. ANIMAL FREEDOM was written across his chest and stomach in black paint. He flipped his tangled locks behind his shoulder and handed me a pamphlet with a caged chicken on it.

"Lo siento, madam," he said to me. "Can I ask if you eat meat?"
I told him I only ate fruit, which, for the moment, was true.
"A fruitarian," he said.
He held up his hands and bowed at my feet.
"That's commitment."
I nodded and agreed that it was.
It didn't take long before I was actually in the van.

Just before I met him, Rat had gone streaking through the parking
lot of a bullfighting arena. The original plan was to get inside like
a fan so he could jump the fence below and run through the actual
ring with pro-animal chants written across his skin, but he lost his
ticket somewhere at a rest stop, and the event was sold out. Rat got
depressed because only a few people had seen him running naked
circles around the parking lot, so Mo and Dirk encouraged him to
keep the slogan on his chest and walk around in a speedo for the
rest of the day in an attempt to get extra actions in.

He'd seemed so noble standing there near-naked in honor of
something bigger than himself. I wanted that, a purpose, something
nonviolent, a set of rules to follow. The We R Animals activists told
me they were headed to Brussels where they would unite with other
vegan activists from London and Paris. I hitched a ride. I think it
made Rat proud, that even though he didn't get to cause a scene
at the bullfighting ring, he had found a new disciple. And Brussels
sounded just as fine as any place to me. Now my choice to fast on
fruit seemed serendipitous, like fate, because here I was in this new

community of activists. They were doing their part to better the world, and I was with them.

They know nothing of what I did to my sister, that I slept with the man she loved in a recliner in her living room. *Why would I do that?* I'm a lesbian for Christ sake. Anything I'm not supposed to have I want. It's like I swallowed a bad seed somewhere. But now I'm thinking maybe the seed can blossom into a flower, a beautiful farm fresh, vegan flower. I can purify myself. The van races toward Brussels, and I wish my period to come so I can add to the reserves in the back. I want to free bleed into an empty bottle. I want to watch myself collect.

Hunger licks my belly with her fire tongue. The roof of my mouth is sore and throbs from excess fructose, but what can I do. I told the vegans I only ate fruit, and that's why they decided to love me, to take me in, so only fruit I will eat. I'm so famished that even the stench can't distract me from my craving. I run a tongue over my furry, starving teeth. I bite into the sword of pineapple Dirk hands me, and the juice cuts my mouth again. Too much fruit, I discover, lands like acid in the gut. I feel a little delirious.

Dirk shows me the scene of an animal slaughterhouse tattooed on his forearm. A cow spews blood from its eyes. Underneath is a fist with a carrot in it, which Dirk explains is the vegan sign of solidarity. I ask him to draw the sign on my forearm with the sharpie they have hanging from the rearview mirror. He obliges, takes my forearm in his lap and concentrates. There is hardly a word to describe how healthy Dirk looks. His body is unpolluted. His veins must pulse special vegan blood. Oh, to glow like Dirk, all apple-cheeked and afro'd. His eyes are so clear, clearer than the sky above us which does not contain a cloud. Maybe my delirium is not delirium but the wind of truth hammering into me. Maybe I have to walk through hunger to get to the other side of myself.

In the front, Rat and Mo brainstorm ideas for new actions.

"Death-in protest in a slaughterhouse."

"Wrap ourselves naked in saran wrap coated with fake blood and package ourselves like meat."

"Use period blood to write help notes from animals on leather jackets. We can use the left hand so the lettering looks like an animal wrote it."

"Write the words DEATH SKIN on fur jackets with ketchup or more blood."

"Lay placentas over the gouda and brie chunks inside a cheese shop."

"Litter the floor of the butcher's shop with teeth."

Dirk suggests the last one with his head still tilted down toward my forearm so he can inscribe me with the vegan sign. Dirk does not look anything like my sister's husband, a retired Latin professor in his late 70s called Bach. But somehow I think of Bach in this moment, think of his bergamot smell and the large hands that had felt soft as the worn pages of a book. Bach is 40 years older than my sister and 50 years older than me, but still, I climbed on top of him that evening and kissed his fuzzy eyebrows. My sister had been away at a lighthouse to study the different colors of the sky for her newest installation. She would paint the sky every day for one month so she could capture each of its many shades. She trusted me to watch her children while she was gone.

My sharpie tattoo is done, and Dirk looks proud. I wonder if his septum ring protects him against some of the van's menstrual stench. I have to look out of the window so I won't just keep staring at Dirk's brown-limbed beauty. He snacks on papaya and I think I, too, should snack on papaya. I should put anything in my mouth that he does because you become what you eat and I would love to become Dirk. I would love to become someone else. His life could look good on me. I could sit in a van, get dragged from city to city, metabolize the death I've been ingesting for years out of me. The next time I see my sister, I could be another person. I have heard that cells regenerate completely every seven years. That means that in only seven years I could be brand-new. Nothing of the old me would remain. I could be like Dirk, regal and sheathed in alarming beauty.

In the front seat, Rat explains to Mo how vegan cum tastes far superior to non-vegan cum. Mo isn't so sure. She says maybe it isn't animal products that foul the cum and turn it smelly but processed food. So, actually vegans who eat processed food might still have smelly semen. Rat seems offended by this hypothesis. He stares at Mo like she punched him.

"No," he says. "It's the flesh of a non-human animal and the milk of a non-human animal that makes the aroma wretched. It's ingesting the non-human animal poison."

We stop at a petrol station near the French border. I walk inside to use the WC. The toilet clerk reminds me of my sister. It's the way she stares at me like she's judging. I hand her my 50 cents, and she examines the coins like they're fake. Her eyes accuse me of something. She pinches her nose like she can smell something bad on my skin. Then again it could be the blood in the van she's smelling. I'm sure it's worked its way into my hair, the cotton of my shirt. On the toilet, I wipe and see hot red clots. Now, I know it's fate. My body is telling me, for once, that I'm in the right place. I wish I could call my sister, text her a picture of the van, a bright orange VW contraption with dog paws drawn on the outside and a shrine to farm animals glued to the dashboard. She would think it was hilarious yet noble. My sister appreciates people with strong convictions, which is why she liked Bach. He'd been jailed for eco-terrorism in the late '80s. He set fire to logging trucks in Northern California and got caught. In prison, he started a school for social justice, a reading group, earned a master's degree in critical race studies, and wrote a book. I wander the candy aisle and look at sweet things that aren't fruit. Chocolate wands and chocolate drops and marzipan. My sister always thought I should find a cause. Something to believe in.

Bach and I had been up late one night. He had been reading Hannah Arendt's *The Life of the Mind*. I'd never heard of Hannah. He started to read her to me: "The sad truth is that most evil is done by people who never make up their minds to be good or evil." That was me! I always ended up doing evil without making the choice. The line stirred me. It dredged up a desire that had settled like sediment on the bottom of my heart. Our eyes met from across the room. I suddenly saw in Bach what my sister saw, a brain pulsing brilliance, shimmering with a critical edge in a world of apathy.

I wanted someone like that to desire me. I wanted Bach to show me I was just as desirable as my sister who painted beautiful sky things and made art from the garbage of the world. Bach and his purple beard and those wool socks with the big toe worn through. I remember how he laid his soft hand on Adorno's *Dialectic of Enlightenment*, as if it were the Bible, as if it could have saved him. I still remember the calloused tip of that big toe.

Somehow, I end up in the cheese aisle. God, those blocks of soft white brie sweating inside their plastic sure look so good. I imagine their salt and mold, the way that chemistry blends together into something utterly good. Dairy. God. A life without dairy. Who can imagine that? The definition of sin. Next to the cheese is a summer sausage. Offensive and flecked with white cellulose spots. I hated having sex with Bach, but I couldn't stop it. I wanted to show my sister that no one was good. Bach wasn't good. Just because he read Hannah Arendt and Angela Davis and Adorno. He could still sleep with a girl 50 years younger than himself in his wife's house while she was in a lighthouse seeking the sky. He could still stuff his old man member inside a younger girl, a lesbian with a mullet and chest binder, in an attempt to feel something. *This is what the youth do. This is youth again.* He didn't even get out of that chair. A lazy boy. He just sat there in his recliner like I was making him, like I was making him like it.

Before I know what I'm doing, I'm peeling back the casing on the summer sausage. My lips quiver. I chew the sausage, and the salt stings the sore spots in my mouth that the fruit made. I am eating that sausage, burping it up, eating it too fast. Then I eat another and another. I could eat them all. And I don't care who's looking. I don't even care.

Fast, Fast, Fast

I do not answer the Wife's calls. Sorry, babe. I am brushing my tongue, watching an internet Pilates video, getting a hot stone massage. Not really. Really, I am scrolling through Ted's Instagram feed. Here is a Portrait of Ted before she had children. Here, a Portrait of Ted with her German husband in Barcelona. Here, a Portrait of Ted with a semi-see-through shirt, a kind of fabric she probably knows the name of—tulle? Chiffon? Voile? Thin cotton lawn? Ted is the kind of woman who knows the specific words for things. Ted is the type of girl who blogs about her fashion choices. I pause on the picture, zoom in. I detect Ted's nipples, a subtle shade of chestnut beneath the sheer fabric. I lie to myself and pretend it's subversive for a woman to objectify another woman. But an object is an object is an object. And I can't stop looking.

Here are many versions of Ted in the just-passed years.

Here, a Portrait of Ted sucking a lollipop. Tongue of hard candy. Sugar in the teeth.

I should answer the Wife's call. Her name overtakes my screen again in sans serif, hoping to FaceTime. It blacks out my Instagram museum. The picture halls of Ted's life become two words which are the name of the person I love. It says THE WIFE. She is the kind of woman who's intelligent about all things with one exception: the emotional lives of others. She could care less about that. Her heart is a cold furnace that only I can heat. The Wife wants to tell me she just landed in Boston for her international law conference.

I text: *You there all safe & sound? Sorry on phone with curator talking about where to position the meat cage.*

The Wife and I are in an open marriage because that is a better arrangement than me cheating on her.

Portrait of Ted getting her first tattoo. Caption: I have tattoos *everywhere.*

That's exactly right. Tattoos. Everywhere. Why does that sound so sexual? Cause she meant it to. You know that. Tattoos cover Ted's arms. They splash color into the crooks of her elbow. A swan opens its wings across her chest as if to fly. A block of cheese sits on her bicep. A chicken roosts on her thigh. Hawk on the fuck-finger. Crossbones on her thumb. The word DADDY on her neck. Each image has that too-fresh patina as if they might still smear. In pictures from a few years ago, Instagram tells me Ted's body was an empty canvas, her haircut an inoffensive blonde bob. Now, a red rat tail pendulums down her neck. A ring has been pierced through the gum above her two front teeth. Her eyes say: *try me, babe.*

I answer the door when Ted knocks. A gust of winter brings her in. We hug in my foyer under a photograph of a serpent eating

a mouse. It's the first time we've seen each other since last month
in my studio when she helped me prepare for my upcoming installation "Fast, Fast, Fast," where I'll re-enact a contemporary take on
Kafka's short story "The Hunger Artist," eating nothing for 14 days,
while confined to a cage made of raw beef. My only task will be to
fill in coloring books with crayons. I was loopy from a 100-hour
practice fast which I broke with a Red Bull and vodka and hot dogs
made of wheat gluten. Ted brought me Harry Potter gummy bears
to celebrate the fast's end. On the cold tile floor, we consumed the
newest flavors: vomit, boogers, dirt, rotten egg, stinky socks. When
she sampled the earwax gummy bear, I stuck my tongue in her ear.
She looked frightened at first, and then pleased. I kept my tongue
there, twirling, twirling, twirling, while she ate her gummy bears
one after the other, giggling.

"It's okay," I told her. "I'm in an open marriage."

"I'm not," she said, meaning no more of that tongue in her ear.

Ted's coat is snowed on. To see her is to feel my palms go slick. There
is a stiffness to our hug. Her spine stands up under my palm. *Why so
nervous?* I think, suspicious of myself. *Be cool.* She smells familiar—
like a kind of essential oil or something one would rub on their wrist
and temples to dissuade a headache from clawing its way into their
brain. It's the smell of a meditation room. Or an acupuncturist's
office. It's the smell of wanting to heal. I want to put my nose against
her eye and inhale. I would like to make love to her ear again, where
that brand-new gauge is stretching out her lobe into a perfect hole-
punched O. She pulls away. She brushes snow onto my floor where

it melts into puddles of water that I will slip on later.

What does Ted want?

Ted tells me the frozen canals outside make the city look like an Avercamp painting. I roll my eyes at the Avercamp namedrop because what a cheesy thing to say.

"I hate Avercamp," I tell her, and she shrugs.

During summer, the city canals stink of something rotten, and boats comb through the ancient waterways, plunging their magnetized arms down in search of sunken bicycles and trash, cleaning out the filth. Once, I sat on a bench smoking an e-cigarette, watching a boat dredge up the garbage. The boat's limb emerged from the black water with a dead body caught in its grip. The human face was molded and fish-eaten, but it seemed to stare right at me. It gave me an idea for a future performance called Death Canal where I would reconstruct a map of Amsterdam with carcasses of rat vermin dressed in tuxedos where the canals should be.

But today the canals are cold, solid things, almost antiseptic. People are walking across them like it's the time of the apocalypse, like Jesus did, walking on water. It seems like an omen. Frozen canals in May. Not good.

Ted runs a finger along a ceramic pot that holds a succulent. The only plant I cannot kill.

"I think you've watered this too much," she says. "It looks bloated and it's shedding its skin."

She means the succulent, which maybe I can kill after all. And thank God she's nervous which I can hear in her voice. It's like I've always said, there's only room for one nervous person in a conversation at a time.

Ted tells me how to care for my succulent and about the problems with her new babysitter (late and rewards screaming toddlers with Netflix cartoons) as she touches all the surfaces of my apartment. She strokes my Bugs Bunny lamp, my stacks of medium format contact sheets, the bottom edge of my David Hockney original, the T-Rex mug I molded with clay. Touch, touch, touch. Her hands are large and undainty. They are hands that make things. They are the hands of a mother.

I know nothing of babies, have never changed a diaper, cannot imagine one sleeping in my house at night. But Ted has two babies, twins named Pin and Fin, little devils that don't sleep at night. I picture Ted's living room, populated by small armies of dinosaurs, broken whole wheat cookies, a carpet emitting the faintest odor of sour milk. The maternal side of her stays mostly hidden, but I get glimpses of it now and then (*here, a tissue for your runny nose, tie your shoes or you're going to trip*), and it sends an electric shock of intrigue to my toes.

"Let's get out of here," says Ted while I rummage the cupboard for two cups, the boiler already cooking tea water.

I had intended for us to relax on the sofa with wimmins-only oolong, to sit holding the steaming cups in our laps, touching them to our collarbones. If we were to fold into the cushions for long enough, if the shadows would slip their blue dresses over our silhouettes, who knows what could happen?

"Oh," I say. "You want to go out?"

She doesn't want to be alone with me here.

I begin to list off the things I've eaten that day in my head. A sign I'm feeling out of control.

BananaYogurtPieceofDarkChocolateHandfulofKettleChips

BananaYogurtPieceofDarkChocolateHandfulofKettleChips.

BananaYogurtPieceofDarkChocolateHandfulofKettleChips.

I should eat less, prepare my body for "Fast, Fast, Fast." The only way to last a full 14 days is to start weaning myself off food, teach my stomach to want little and then nothing. But my self-control is basically non-existent.

"Cookie?" I say, holding up a Delft blue tin of butter sweets I bought from the tourist shop down the road. "You don't want a cookie first?"

"Well if you want me to take an artist photo, it's better to do it outside and soon. The light. It's—"

She holds her fingers up in a way that signals *OK* instead of just saying it. The rays of winter slant toward the window behind her, the perfect texture, the pure touch of blue.

Fucking artist photos.

Had I forgotten this had been the plan? Or had I hoped that she had forgotten? I don't even need new headshots. I love the one I have now where it looks like I'm growling right at the camera, a deranged look sitting in my eye, my upper lip snarled like I want to bite you. I figured Ted had known what I meant, that my request was just an excuse for us to hang out, maybe become intimately connected. I don't even like her photographs—who does? People should be better at reading minds. I'm serious about that.

I open the front door for Ted and make a gesture that means *after you, my lady*, but now that I know she can't read minds, who knows what she thinks I mean. Winter rushes toward us. Ted runs a hand across the flannel of my stomach as she passes through the archway she just entered minutes ago. It's always like this, as soon as we're in a safe zone, a public street, straight girls get all flirty. I'm almost annoyed but then she turns her head toward me, and I see that she applied makeup before she came over. The layer of foundation runs across her cheeks. The glimmer of green above her eyes. A hard kohl edge to the bottom of her lids. I'm touched by the gesture, though I'm sure she puts on makeup every day for everyone, there is still something vulnerable in witnessing a woman trying to make themselves more beautiful to the world. I soften.

"You remind me of my best friend from high school," she tells me as we walk.

Key word here—*friend*. Real subtle, Ted. But this is one of the themes I'm interested in in my next performance: the way we project connections we've had in the past onto the new people we meet. We thread feelings from one person to the next until they are all wound up in the same knotted ball of string until we can't disentangle who they are from who we expected them to be. I've already come up with a name for that performance: "Knot So Many Knot So Sure."

"Tell me about your friend," I say.

Ted just scrunches up her face, shrugs. Sometimes there's too much to tell. I've had many different types of friends. One such friend and I spent every night of high school dry humping each other in her twin bed while the constellation Canis Major, arranged in plastic stars, watched from the ceiling. That kind of friend, Ted?

On the street, swans hobble along the sides of the frozen canals, castaway from their homes which have been transformed into skating rinks. Parrots fly overhead, exotic green birds that shiver through the air, migrating from park to park. Red-faced men with chicken pox scars and drunk, detached eyes sell hot chocolate to children. They leer. Mothers lead their white-haired babies down to the edge of the ice where they slip and fall but do not drown. A woman whose chin has disappeared into her neck tries to get someone to buy a pair of old ice skates.

When I first moved to Amsterdam, I found it hard to live around so much water. With water, there is never stillness. There is motion, a current, somewhere always a ripple, somewhere always a tide. The canals travel like arteries through the city, pulsing and beating and flooding it with movement. Each day, I would swim backward through the city's salted sea-brain. I would sink into a bathtub until my fingerprints pruned. I would close my eyes to think and feel the black sea bulging over the sides of the dikes, crashing in wild, windswept waves onto the western coast, gasping toward land, until one day there would be nothing that wasn't covered by the sea's sodden palm. For years, I felt as though my brain had drowned. I could not think. It was raining in my interior lobe, a constant dreary drizzle. Clouds moved together and wept fog into my hippocampus. I blinked away the condensation which clouded everything in a watery blur.

I longed for a harsh dry heat. I wanted to sit on a parched desert floor where the sun had cracked open the ground, daring it to breathe. I wanted to burn so bad I got melanoma. I wanted to feel the sun cook the meat of me. The water continued to rise in the city. It rose. It swilled. It leaked out of my mouth.

But now that winter has sucked condensation from the air and stilled the canals into something as hard as a marble floor, now that icicles hang like teeth on the sides of awnings, threatening to break off and impale you, now that snow covers everything like a still Siberian plain, I miss the water. I take my first full breath in years and realize just that. It's typical behavior. This insatiable wanting of the thing I cannot have.

The Wife does not have a powerful sex drive. It's not about sex, the open marriage. It's about another type of desire, something deeper than sex—something closer to obsession. You see, I cannot act normally around the people I like, friend or otherwise. I cannot meet someone interesting and just be chill. When I like someone, I become a train steaming downhill without brakes. The Wife has come to accept this. With Ted, I think the seed of the intrigue started on the night I first met her, at our mutual friend's wedding reception in Westerfabriek. Her husband had been brooding in the corner eating sausage and talking to a graphic designer who considered the logos he made for internet brands "art." Ted had come to me because she recognized me from my "It's Not Me, It's Me" exhibition last year. The show had been a flop. The papers hated it, and I lost my agent. Even I knew the show was a failure and poorly executed, but I could tell from Ted's coy little expression that she thought it was brilliant. Ted, standing there with her plastic plate of crudités, how just like a woman. Of course, she liked the show. She didn't know what good was. She dressed just like everyone else but better. She seemed to suck all the hope and goodness in the room toward her. I'm serious. Everything else was dim compared to Ted. Life seemed to be kicking around inside of her, looking for a way out. Me? Was I the way out? Was I life? Then Ted laughed, covered her mouth with her big hand, and I saw her swallow a word instead of saying it, and I thought: *What word? What word did you swallow, Ted?*

Ted has me lean against the wrought iron railing of a bridge, a scene of ice skaters behind me. Idyllic. The worst scene ever for artist photos. Oh, Christ. I will never use this.

"Smile," she says. "Smile big."

Her confidence is mesmerizing. *Remember that,* I tell myself. Remember that if you are confident enough people will believe almost anything to be true. They will love your art forever if you just exude a bit more conviction.

Ted takes a photo of me looking tickled, a photo of my chin resting on my fist, a photo of me throwing my hands over my head like the world is without suffering. Maybe this will be a good photo. Maybe Ted sees me more clearly than anyone else.

Maybe, maybe, maybe.

I hate that word.

"Here," she says.

She walks right up to me so that I can smell her essential oils. She moves a tangle of hair behind my ear. When she smiles, the piercing on her gums says hello.

"Just like that," she says. "So pretty, you."

A compliment, how I love those. I want to crawl into her arms. I let her look me right in the eye. Her eyes are paragraphs typed in a foreign language. If I could, I would upload her expression into Google Translate. What does it even mean?

"You," she says. "You, you, you."

"You," I say back. My voice is low and not my own. "You."

Something is going to happen. Snow falls around us like we're a scene glued to the bottom of a shaken globe.

"Me," I say, and my voice is mine again.

Then we hear it. The noise mechanic I used to share a studio with in the USA told me ice sounds like aliens singing when it breaks. He had an iPhone full of those eerie reverberations. He'd traveled to Minnesota, Vermont, Alaska to capture the ice shifting and melting and splitting open. It sounds like a lightsaber slicing through the air, not at all what one might imagine. That's how I know what is happening before my eyes even grab the image. I hear the aliens singing. I hear the lightsaber unsheathed and soaring. Ted screams. I turn and look at the canal behind me, and I see it, the whole canal filled with people—mothers and children, fat men and bent grandmothers gripped by horror—as the ice below them shifts and breaks and cries right open. The ice is teeth inside a jaw that wants to swallow them. There they go, the bodies, into the black water alive and vicious and waiting to eat them. Waiting to swallow them down that frozen, heart-stopping throat. *Oh God*, I think. Ted takes my hand and holds it to her heart. Her heart is loud against my palm. Her heart is kicking me. I look at her, and she takes my picture. I'm not smiling, who could smile, when so many people are drowning.

Possum

When I visited the rainy city, I went to a small, light-filled studio and had my astrological birth chart read. The woman was a Leo with dark blue eyes and perfect posture. She had the haircut I wanted, and I found myself caring more about if she thought I was interesting than what she was saying about the way the sky looked the night I was born. I was born in the season of Cancer. Right after the solstice. The warmest time of the year. It's the season to swim outside. It's the season to sit in the sun and burn. The Leo looked into my eyes and told me I was special just like I hoped she would.

I was getting my birth chart read because I needed guidance, and I wanted to hear someone tell me things about myself. I wanted to know why I kept coming back to the rainy city to roam and wander and stick pins into my heart.

While I was in the rainy city, I met a possum. A record skipped in my chest. The possum was a song I didn't want to stop playing.

The possum and I started talking about spirit guides, and it made me curious about the stars—if Saturn was returning and if that was why I was wandering the streets with my eyes pressed into dark corners and down alleys and into cleavage I shouldn't be seeing.

I hoped the Leo astrologer would take my hand and divine my future from it. I hoped she would tell me she saw my future and the possum was in it. I thought maybe the possum would turn over the garbage can of my life and eat out all the trash. But the Leo did not see the possum in my stars. She did not see the possum at all.

The possum was a fire sign, and it showed in how she removed her clothes even on cold days and walked through the air conditioner sweating. Her hair had an orange tinge to it like a flame or like the sun. She was something I wanted to touch but couldn't.

Ever since Halloween, when I had a very innocent, very casual dirty dancing session with the possum in our mutual friend's living room, I've wanted the possum. The wanting was a shake that started in my toenails and moved up toward something that wasn't my brain. The night ended two minutes before we would have been making out. Some might call that fate. Or a cosmic intervention.

I didn't live in the rainy city when I met the possum. I was only visiting, but the possum made me wonder if moving back to the rainy city might be a great idea.

The possum told me, "If you lived here we would get into a lot of trouble."

The way the possum said *trouble* made me want to have it. It made me want to eat drugs from the palm of her hand and follow her down the interstate on a motorcycle at 4 a.m. I wanted to turn a dollar into a straw and suck the possum up my nose.

The possum said, "You have the twinkle of mischief in your eye."

The possum and I came up with many reasons to see each other and only canceled once in a while. I would find excuses to touch her possum skin. I would brush against her elbow to get her attention or sit so close that our knees had to kiss at the bone. I wanted to tuck the possum's hair behind her ear while we talked, but I was afraid to do that, so I told the possum how I wanted a spirit guide and someone to pray to. The possum had been going to Hare Krishna meetings and used to rise at dawn to drink the wind of God. So, she understood my desire to see things that weren't there.

I told the possum about my Puerto Rican great-grandmother who lived to be 115 and had special powers to heal people in her village. I told the possum that the Leo astrologer said I needed to obtain a talisman from my great-grandmother, an old object, something to take with me, carry in my pocket, stroke in the bright sun. The astrologer told me I should start praying to my grandmother, write her letters, ask her for something.

The possum said, "I thought so. I thought you should do that, too."

The new moon was going to be in Gemini. We wrote out manifestations. For my last manifestation, I wrote: fuck a possum.

Then I crossed it out.

The possum went to a psychic, and the psychic told her some things but not other things. I wanted the psychic to tell the possum about me, to tell her that she should spend the evening in the park running her possum tongue across my shins. But that's not what happened. The psychic told the possum things that were sensible and vague.

"Nothing is going on," the possum told our friends when they asked.

I would sit next to the possum and get very wet. Just sitting next to the possum made my body burn. She could have slid right in, but she didn't.

When my back was hurting, the possum let me lay my head in her lap, and she played with my hair as the sun melted into the rooftops around us. When we went on a walk she put her fingers in her pockets so I knew not to hold her hand. We were geocaching on a bridge near a homeless tent encampment, and the rainy city sign was glowing and blinking above us, and it was almost midnight and she stopped to take a picture of it. She got so excited when we found the tiny geocache object that I wanted to find another geocache just to see the possum smile like that again. The next time we were supposed to see each other the possum could not make it, and I knew why.

We decided that meditating would be an important part of our spiritual journeys. The possum said, "One of the reasons I like talking to you is that you get what I mean when I say I'm searching for something."

The possum told me, "I want to tell you how I feel?"

I said, "About?"

The possum said, "About you."

We had a date to meditate in a graveyard, but the possum never came.

I felt like this once for a Canadian who I met at a campground on Highway 101. Somewhere on the rugged coast, we hitched tents side by side and that was that. The Canadian made me feel insane. I wanted to buy her boxes of flowers that girls in skirts on bikes would deliver right to her door. I did extraordinary things to sit next to her at the dinner table. I crossed seas on ferry boats. I jumped into frigid lakes naked in November. I knew how to be the cool girlfriend, how to make my feelings so small she wouldn't even notice they're there.

I did that with the possum, too. The feeling thing. I was a neon sign of attention. Online for the possum at all times.

And I lied about something already.

The possum and I kissed once. On Halloween. It was the kind of kiss that feels like it never happened so maybe it never did. Maybe we were too drunk to remember. Maybe that's the same thing. The possum walked right up to me while I was staring into my drink in a corner. She intimidated me, and that rarely happens, so of course I paid attention. The possum was exuberant, danced with a freedom that came from somewhere far away. I wanted to be far way with her. Everyone was kissing. Friends were kissing friends because there were ghosts and demons to exorcise and a haunted night to enjoy. Our kiss might have been nothing more than that: a celebration between two people who were just friends.

The possum said, "Thanks for dancing with me tonight."

Across the room, I watched a lion twerk toward a scarecrow. I watched a zombie light the end of a bong.

The Leo astrologer told me, "Next month you should expect emotional turbulence. Transformation is not glamorous. It's actually very painful and very hard."

The next time I visit the rainy city, I stand with the possum in the middle of the street and it's summer. Above us, the constellations fix the fate of people being born in places we can't see, and we are just here. The possum has a look in her eye like she's glimpsed the dark soul of the universe. She is holding my secrets, and they are kicking in her fist. I see them in her arm outstretched above her head, just out of reach. I think she has kept a piece of me, and I wonder if that means I will remember her or if she will remember me. I don't know, because I've never loved a possum and I probably never will. But this came close. Oh, so close.

Cultural Relativism

The heat here rots the flowers. Petals lay like swathes of torn silk in the grass. This, they tell me, is summer in Alabama. Everything the sun can kill it does. So, I spend my mornings grading papers by the pool. That calm square of chlorine numbs my mind. I watch a woman rip a toddler from the kiddie pool by his chubby arm. Two vanilla pudding–colored boys stalk a girl into the deep end.

I remind myself why I came here, to this small, withered town in the middle of the South's saddest state. Experience. A great job at a decent university. And also, as I told Frieda, if I didn't leave Amsterdam soon, I was going to become a monster.

I needed change. I missed my dead brother.

Before I left Amsterdam, I was still pondering—to go to Alabama or not to go. Frieda said, "Go."

"You can do good there," Frieda said. "In Alabama."

Her German accent had made Alabama sound exotic. It was like she tricked me.

My office is pinched between sorority row and fraternity drive, and the landscaping is maintained with an almost erotic precision. The campus combined the fanfare of football with a dark Faulkner gloom in a beautiful way. Conjure something that looks ivy league—colonial mansions, wide lawns shaved to the height of an army crew cut, phallic chimes, Gothic revival buildings, Ionic columns. Now, bring in a vicious Southern sun and burn everything so it walks with a limp. There, perfect.

On the walk to my classroom, I pass the frat boys. They loaf in their lawn chairs as if they are kings. Their hair falls slovenly across their eyes, and their clothes conjure a specific kind of preppy. When I see them, I smell wet socks. They look like bad copies of my brother. They come to my class late with Greek lettering sewn to the front of their shirts. Greek, as if they were another nationality—or worse, as if they were mythical beings. They always bring something loud to class to interact with: a bag of chips that needs to be torn open, a crisp apple that requires a bite, a cold whose forceful release comes in the shape of constant coughing. They call me ma'am as if I asked for it.

After class, a boy with a tie-dye shirt lingers by his desk. His droopy eyes are cast to the linoleum. He says he wants to ask me a question about cultural relativism.

I tell the boy, "Let's walk and talk."

We walk past the building where, in 1963, the state governor stood in order to prevent racial integration on the university campus. I ask the boy if he knows the significance of the auditorium. He stares back at me, caressing his hemp necklace.

110

"Kind of," he says. "I've seen the pictures."

"They didn't teach you about it in high school?" I ask.

"Might have," he says, as if he can't remember.

I don't know why I'm even asking him about his education. I know it was lacking. I checked out an old high school history textbook from the library before the semester started, looking to confirm my suspicion about bias in education. Low and behold, I discovered a passage detailing slavery as the first form of social security in the US. The text said something about how slaves were provided with food and medical attention free of charge. I could hardly believe it. Of course, I sent a photo of the text to Frieda right away. LIES! I wrote. The book went on to describe how slaves were considered part of the owner's family and often treated as such. *Ongelofelijk*, I muttered to myself, flipping through the musty pages. *Unbelievable* always sounded more staggering when I said it in Dutch.

A task force of white sorority girls staggers past us, their long teeth flashing as they shriek gossip from the previous night. They smell like drowned dogs, a scent so strong it punches through the screen of perfume slathered over their skin. The boy appears scared of them, and his fear endears me to him.

Above us, the cloudless blue sky rains down heat. We pass the Episcopalian church where, in the 1960s, KKK members came in white robes and torched crosses on the lawn because the church allowed a black student to attend its service. They did this in the light of day. At least three of them were professors at the university. These monuments of horror are hidden on every plain-looking corner. I see an elderly man attempting to wheel an elderly woman across the crosswalk. Each time he tries to step into the road a car careens past. Jesus, I think. This man trying to help his wife across the road is the last sad straw on my back of sadness.

Frieda sends me a selfie of herself pooping. I see the black walls of the bathroom behind. The familiar pink graffiti scribbled across the stall. *No Human Is ILLEGAL. Geen Vlees is Diervriendelijk.* I miss Amsterdam, where, in this very moment, it's the hot and sticky center of the night. I wonder who, if anyone, Frieda will take home. She always had a thing for the Harvard-dropout poet who wore an XL dog collar as a belt. My missing runs so deep it isn't even a feeling anymore. It's become my essence.

When we get to my office, the boy with the tie-dye shirt reminds me that his name is RJ. He tells me he wants to major in literature—that is what he wants to talk about.

"I thought you wanted to talk about cultural relativism," I say, putting my phone on airplane mode in case Frieda gets a wild hair and wants to send an even seedier photo, like a tit pic or a full nude.

"Maybe, I want to major in literature so I can continue to ask more questions about cultural relativism," says RJ.

"Uh huh," I say. "What's really on your mind?"

"Have you read *In Cold Blood*?" says RJ.

"Sure," I say. "A classic."

"I want to write the next *In Cold Blood*," says RJ.

He crosses his skateboard shoes in front of him. He moves a flock of bang from his eyes and stares at me with a look I know means: I have a secret. In high school, I must have had a crush on a boy like RJ—a boy so naive the only way he could think to rebel was to become a hippie, a way of life he probably discovered in his granddad's record collection. A plastic baggy of shrooms is no doubt stuffed deep in his jean pocket. His I-care-too-much-to-care swagger is oddly familiar.

"You do?" I say. "Well, maybe you should sign up for a creative writing class."

"I guess, uh," he says, "it's because I need to process something."

Outside, the sororities are preparing for the first football game of the season. Their chorus rises as they fight over what kind of crimson tissue they should use for the parade floats they're making. Slices of conversation drift into my office window. Their sentences are stuffed with sad, sleepy words missing r's and leaking vowels. I fight back the urge to wrench my neck to the side so that it cracks, a tick I have noticed makes people squeam.

"And what's that," I ask, "that you need to process?"

"My friend murdered someone," he says casually, as if he were shrugging a shoulder.

"Murdered," I say, my blood turning cold just like the title RJ invoked.

I glance at his backpack, remembering that American teenagers sometimes have guns.

"It's not a secret," he says. "It's all over the papers. My friend Tyler killed his mother this summer. He shot her in the stomach, and now he's probably going to jail."

"Probably going to jail or—?"

"I mean he's out on probation, staying out at his uncle's farm, but he doesn't seem, you know, sorry or anything. Even though, well, his life is like ruined."

"Why are you telling me this?" I ask.

"Well," says RJ. "The books you're having us read. All kinds of bad stuff happens in them."

He says this to me as if this answers my question.

"I see," I say.

But really, I don't see. I see a sad boy whose friend killed his mother, and I'm wondering what's in his bag.

"Do you want me to refer you to someone that you can talk to about this?"

"I am talking about it," says the boy, shifting in his chair. "To you."

You can't un-hear something once you've heard it, my dad used to say. And he is right. All I can hear now is *my friend shot his mother in the stomach inthestomach inthestomach.*

"He wasn't a bad guy," says RJ.

I nod.

"I don't know why he did it. He didn't harm animals or anything. I didn't even know he had a gun, but he did. A sawed-off shotgun."

"I see," I say.

"See?" he asks.

"Uh huh," I say.

And I refer RJ to the counselor.

I stop to buy Big Red gum and vitamin water at the gas station. The man behind the counter is smoking. I eye his nasal catheter as he hands me my change, a crumpled American fiver that still looks like Monopoly money to me. That's what living abroad for years does to you, familiar things start to take on a strangeness.

The man rasps at me, "You take care, ma'am. All right, all right."

That stops me. I look up at the man, his hard, metal-colored eyes.

"How are you today?" I ask him.

"Could be better," he says. "Getting over some cancer treatment but—"

He waves his hand as if mentioning a heat wave that would pass soon.

"I'm so sorry," I say, realizing this word is traveling out of my throat too often these days.

"Well." The man shrugs. "You have a good one, ma'am," he says, and I see he's the one trying to make me feel better.

I text Frieda about the hippie boy with the murderer friend. I try to make a joke out of it—another unhinged white man on the loose! —but really it troubles me. I keep seeing RJ's eyes skittering over my bookshelf like he wanted to export his memories into a ream of pages bound in hardcovers like the ones lined up on my office wall. I could understand the impulse. When I moved to Amsterdam, I had been running from something, hoping my dissertation could act as a funnel in which the trauma of my brother's death could be rerouted into something productive. I had written about metaphors of violence in Southern literature.

I stop outside the Sigma Nu fraternity house—nay, mansion—
and gaze up at it. The building sits far back on the lawn and the
windows are so small that the only thing I can see from the street
are warm squares of light that hint at occupancy. My brother died
in a hazing accident. That's what they called it: an accident. As if
his future fraternity brothers hadn't demanded that he jump from
a bridge into a cold river at midnight, into a current that moved
so fast its frothy caps could be seen from three stories up where
my brother shook and trembled on the bridge's rail. He landed on
a piece of plywood and snapped his neck. This was after weeks of
drinking the pee of his future frat brothers, waking up at dawn to
make their girlfriends breakfast, and, I kid you not, licking vomit
from the fraternity carpet after a party to clean it.

I tell Frieda over Skype how RJ actually looks like my brother. I
didn't realize it until the next day when I saw him in class.

"Well," says Frieda. "Maybe the ghost of your brother has
implanted himself in RJ and is coming back to tell you he's okay."

"You're saying he chose the body of a boy whose friend killed his
mother to tell me things are okay?"

"Okay, you're right," said Frieda. "That'd be a weird choice. But
your brother does sound like he was a dark fellow. No offense."

"Offense not taken," I say.

"We both know you only moved to Alabama to be closer to him.
So, it's only fitting that you're seeing him in your students."

"Um," I say, knowing she's right.

My brother had enrolled at the University of Alabama and fallen in love with what he called the traditions of the South. And then those traditions killed him.

I tell her I spent the entire afternoon diving down the rabbit hole of court documents. Tyler told the police he and his mother had been fighting because Tyler's mother was sleeping with a boy his age that went to his high school. He said his mother had pulled a fork from the drawer and stabbed him in the stomach with it three times. Then she made him wash the fork with the rest of the dishes piled up in the sink. Later that night, he walked into the living room where she was watching TV and shot her in the abdomen.

"I got the chills," says Frieda. "That sounds like something from *American Horror Story*."

"I can't get out the image of him washing the fork," I say.

"I can't get out the image of him shooting his mother in the stomach," says Frieda.

"Well," I say. "Yeah."

Frieda says she can't talk long because she's starring in an underground retelling of *Zanna, Don't!* I'm about to ask if the poet is going, but then I think—what's the point? What's the point of telling Frieda anything. She puts me on hold because she's buying a salad at the grocery store. I listen to the static of her coat pocket, the garbles of Dutch pleasantries—if there was such a thing—and close my eyes. If I close my eyes and listen, it's like I am still there. The hair stands up on my arms as if it can feel the fresh Nordic hair. Since moving to Alabama, I take a cardigan with me everywhere, even though I know I won't need it. I stare at the bunched-up piece of outerwear in my hand and throw it at the wall of my office.

"Well, have fun tonight," I tell Frieda.

I create a Google alert for Tyler's trial. His court date is approaching. With a little digging, I find an address for a man who lives in the country with his same last name. His uncle, if you ask me. I record the address in my phone. *What am I doing?*

Capote writes: "There's got to be something wrong with us. To do what we did."

That's from *In Cold Blood*. I keep thinking of that line as I walk through campus to my office. Then back across campus to my classroom. I think of all the bad things that happened right here on this campus, in the rural land around in. There must be something wrong.

I drive out to the address in my phone. I pass trailer homes and pastures strewn with rolls of hay. An angry sun boils in the distance. It looks hard as a nickel. I burrow deeper into the country until the only buildings I see are churches and gas stations and trailers. The signs are strange.

What you weave on Earth, you wear in Heaven, one tells me.
Go to Church or the Devil Will Get You, says another.
Tide Rolled.
#Secede.

I pause in front of the mailbox I think belongs to Tyler's uncle. What do I expect to find? The road disappears into the woods. Crows circle above the tops of trees as if there's something dead

back there. My hands are shaking on the steering wheel. At the end
of the road, I imagine a house painted farmer red, a shed filled with
tools, a garden that grows wholesome things like kale and carrots
and two men on the porch talking about redemption, guns laying
on their laps.

Just drive home, I tell myself.

I don't know why I need to see Tyler. What will it prove? I've
already seen his mugshot online. He looks so average that I might
miss him in a crowd. A shaved head of brown hair. Almond eyes
with blank green centers. His mouth turns down like his aura is a
frown. There was no attitude in his expression. The picture could
have been taken on any old afternoon. I imagine Tyler not shooting
his mother, but matriculating in the university instead and joining a
fraternity and taking his unused rage out on RJ or an unsuspecting,
eager pledge. I imagine Tyler taking his pledge to a bridge, saying,
"Jump, coward, jump if you want our love."

I get out of the car, squat, and piss next to my tire. There's
nobody out here. The fields run away from me in all directions.
Somewhere in them, Tyler is walking like a free man.

RJ writes a story and wants me to read it. In the story, a boy named
Skyler kills his sister and instead of going to jail he is sent to a mili-
tary-style ranch for cowboys who have lost their way. At the ranch,
they must make their beds and exercise and march in thick jackets
in the boiling afternoon. The boys must pray, and the prayers work.
The character Skyler is healed. He's released back to the world with
a heart full of hope. He becomes a painter and paints portraits of

young girls and their families.

I tell RJ his story is good. He submits it to the school literary journal where it wins second place in an undergraduate competition. Fall erases summer. Football season begins, and then it ends. Tyler gets 20 years in the state prison for manslaughter. Only 20 years for matricide, I think. I don't believe in the death penalty, but the sentence seems short to me, as if killing your mother can be forgiven by spending 20 years in a cage. Who knows, maybe it can.

It's springtime, and the weather is lovely. The sky is cloudless, and snow never comes like it does in Amsterdam. I don't talk with Frieda anymore, though I do text her to tell her about Tyler's sentence.

"Retribution," she texts back.

I don't think I'll see RJ again until I do. I glimpse him across the street. He looks the same but different. He's still wearing tie-dye. I walk into a store selling university T-shirts to hide from him. Unexpected encounters unsettle me. The entire store is hung with crimson cloth and images of elephants. I feel like I've walked into a menstrual pad.

I want to text Frieda, "Look, the school's color is red like period blood."

But I text nothing.

On the way to my classroom, where I will teach Survey of Southern Literature, I stop in front of a frat house and pluck a daisy from the ground. I imagine a future where I'm teaching RJ's novel. It will be about a boy who shoots his mother, an elementary school teacher and a single mom, in cold blood, in the stomach, right above the womb that grew him. I will explain to the class what Southern Gothic is. I will talk about trauma in the South, how it runs so deep, how it's in the soil. I will explain that we drink the violence in like water from the tap. We take big gulps of it that we think will nourish us until we're made up of the violence, until it's in our very cells.

Scarecrow

"Eat the worm," said Jed. The camera's viewfinder was pushed against his glasses.

Crow looked down at the wet pink body in her hand. Wiggle, wiggle went the worm. It was as slimy as a stomach, a snot rocket, an eye. Jed came over with a fishing can full of them. He wanted to light fire to them, sprinkle them with salt, put them on bread.

"Eat it, eat it, eat it," said Jed.

"You crazy," said Crow.

"What you think, Little Joey?" asked Jed.

Little Joey went, "Fun."

Of course, Little Joey thought it was fun. Little Joey's nine-year-old face was glazed as always, blinking slow, moving his lips over his teeth so slow. Crow thought Little Joey was either a future genius or a future serial killer. She hadn't figured out which yet. She eyed him. That hatchet stuck in his belt loop. The blade was rusted but still sharp.

Little Joey dropped the worm in the red room of his mouth. His teeth were fang-like, as if someone had shaved them into peculiar points, but Crow was pretty sure it was natural, as natural as the color of his skin, which was pale enough to look blue. In the bright sun, that's how he appeared, like a vein-colored boy eating worms in the afternoon while two teenagers stared.

Crow went to Jed's house, but he was not home. Jed's father, who Crow never heard him mention once, had picked him up and taken him gun shopping. Jed and Little Joey's mother told Crow that Little Joey was home if she wanted to play with him while she waited for Jed.

Crow did not suggest that she was too old to play. Their mom was always a little jittery, like she expected something to jump out and scare her. She leaned against the door to let Crow pass. Crow found Little Joey alone in the living room. The blinds buried the light.

"I'm waiting for Dead," said Little Joey when she asked what he was up to. Dead was what he called his half-brother, a symptom of the speech impediment that twisted up his words.

Smoke from the mother's cigarettes produced a house-wide cloud so dense and unrelenting that Crow broke out in a rash along her neck, developed a wet cough that her lungs drove out.

"Can I turn on a light?" asked Crow.

Crow inherited a video camera from her uncle, who died unexpectedly from a cause Crow's family wouldn't talk about. When her uncle was alive, he showed her how to shoot a rifle at a deer and how to shoot a camera at a person. Crow began to carry a notebook in her front pocket, just like he did, so she could record her observations as she saw them. Her uncle was a Pentecostal, hill pastor, who believed the US government was involved in corruption scandals like orchestrating the attack on the twin towers on 9/11 and painting chemical trails across the sky that leaked poison on common people and affected the weather. After her uncle died, people found his bedroom walls covered with mind maps detailing how federal agencies put poison in impoverished people's drinking water in an attempt to eradicate poverty by killing the poor. He'd accumulated these ideas from his internet trawls. She'd felt moved by his rigor, the way he continued to hunt down the truth even if no one else believed him.

Her uncle taught her how to speak in tongues when she was only ten. They went down to the river behind his house. He gripped a Bible in both hands and stretched it toward the cloudless blue sky, toward Heaven itself. She fell into the mud bank before him and shook. She spoke in rhymed, blank, and free verses. Her eyes pulled back in her head until only the whites shown. She shook and shook, and her uncle danced like someone struck with the spirit. Now, she isn't sure if what she felt was really God or if she'd wanted it to be so bad she made it so. She got a white scar on her chin from all that flailing on the ground she did that day. She named it her God Mark. Speaking tongues never happened again even though sometimes she asked God for it, the gift of his language. She begged God in her brain, but her words only ever came out in English. Maybe it was something from her uncle that slipped inside of her that day. Maybe he gave her the strength to reach out and bite into those strange sounds that had been shifting through the air. In the last years of her uncle's life, she'd hardly heard a word from him. No one had. That's why she was surprised when her mom told her he had left her his camera and seven boxes filled with film.

Crow's first project was to make a documentary about skateboarding in Alabama. She loved the click-click-whirr of the camera catching the action. The film would star Jed, but Little Joey crept in more and more lately. Little Joey was fearless. It was a superpower. It was the kind of things that could make a person famous—that could make a documentary get seen. He back-flipped off concrete stairs on cue. He drove his board off ramps pulled to the edge of a dark lake. When Jed said, "Drop in on that half-pipe and do some crazy shit, Little Joey," Little Joey abided, and Crow would film him fling his limbs to the sky. Little Joey fell, sure, but he got up again.

Crow's mother said, "I feel bad for that little one. He's not going to have a brain to speak. He's hit that head of his about more times than I can count."

Crow said, "Yeah."

Because it was true.

"But medicine is real advanced," said Crow. "Doctors can probably fix him if he does himself in bad."

Little Joey cleaved gashes into his chin but hardly an emotion eclipsed his face. After each fall, he dusted himself off and stared like a sociopath at Jed, who would sip his 7 Up and clap. Once he swallowed a tooth whole. The tooth came out later when Little Joey pooped in the toilet. He pulled the tooth from the bowl, bleached it, and begun to carry it around in a miniature Crown Royal bag.

Jed made Crow film as he kicked soccer balls at Little Joey's face while Little Joey stood still in the middle of the yard with his eyes peeled open. Two out of three balls hit him right in the skull, but he just took it. Ball after ball after ball. He didn't even flinch.

"You hate him or something?" Crow had asked. "You got to stop. I'm not going to film a second more."

But Jed acted like it was his decision to stop kicking balls at his brother, whose eyes had turned red and wet from the pain inflicted upon him.

"Come here and give me a hug, you brave-ass fucker," said Jed.

Little Joey ran right up to him and burrowed his snot-smeared face in his brother's stomach, and the two boys shrieked.

Wherever Jed and Crow went, so too went Little Joey. It helped that Jed was cool. His coolness came to him naturally, the way some people are tall or have perfectly round biceps or a dimple on either side of their smile. Crow recognized his coolness and understood that it gave him a certain power. If Jed arrived at school wearing black socks up to his knees, the next day, other boys would wear their socks the same way. He stuck a safety pin through his ear and so did a girl in his math class. He burned the word ROCK into his forearm with the metal tip of a lighter and two boys singed geometric shapes into their knuckles.

Jed was the only person in the world Crow could stand to be around all day long. Everyone at school called Crow a lesbian, but

Crow was positive she was not a lesbian because she was in love with Jed. She liked the way he grew his sideburns long. She thought the sneezes crusted below his nose were cute. The gummy scar that ran the length of his forearm was something she wanted to touch with more than her eyes.

Crow sat at the skate park with her legs open and her shoulders hunched. Her hair was just like Jed's: a flop of curls that hung in her face. Sometimes her mother snapped back some of her hair with a butterfly barrette, but it looked silly paired with her polo shirts, cargo shorts, and jet-black Nike Airs. She hung a chain from the pockets of her pants and a skeleton key around her neck that she found on the ground of an abandoned mill. She buttoned her shirts all the way up to her Adam's apple. She wanted to follow Jed anywhere. He was an enigma to her—a mystery wrapped in a riddle.

"Crow is lesbo, even if she don't know," called a girl from the bed of truck.

"Bitch, I'll show you what a man is," said a neighbor from his stoop. His stomach sat large and quivering on his lap.

"Crow, you exactly like a boy," said Jed, but he said it with love.

So much like a guy, he said, that he regularly forgot she was a girl at all, except that she was afraid to swim in the same pool with him at the same time because Crow didn't know exactly how a girl got pregnant. She'd learned that technically the penis had to enter into the woman's vagina and ejaculate for a baby to start to grow. But Crow's aunt told her differently. Her aunt told her that she got pregnant when she was fourteen from mutually masturbating with her boyfriend. Crow didn't want to risk anything. She thought maybe sperm could travel alive from Jed's penis and swim through the chlorine toward her. She, unlike Little Joey, had been born with the fear gene. She was a scared cat. A scarecrow. Which was what Jed started calling her years ago, which was how she got the nickname Crow.

On the afternoon Crow got her first tattoo, she walked into the skate park to find Jed with his shirt peeled off and his skeletal frame sunk into a lawn chair, waiting. The sun hid behind a sheet of clouds. The heat was wet and mean. It was like a wall you had to walk through. A six-pack of 7 Up sat beside Jed. Some skaters ripping it up on the half-pipe had stopped to watch Little Joey. Little Joey's spills looked somehow more impressive than the technical moves Jed could complete helmetless with nothing but a pair of black JNCOs, a dog collar, and a strung-out white shirt.

Late. Jed checked his watch and tapped his wrist to emphasize it. Crow showed Jed the line from an E. E. Cummings poem she had inscribed just under the collarbone. Fresh ink and blood. Heat and fire tingle. Her mother took her as a present for turning sixteen. Jed raised an eyebrow like *who cares.*

"Well?" She asked, nonchalant, as if she didn't care what he thought.

"Kind of cheesy as all hell, don't you think?" said Jed.

"You're jealous because you don't have one."

"Whatever," said Jed. "You'll know it when I'm jealous."

But Crow was right. Jealous was what he was, jealous she didn't let him stick-and-poke a monster into her bicep with needles he bought from the thrift store. She refused to hold a cigarette to her stomach while he held one to his so that their skin would melt into matching skin scars. Jed had reams of notebooks filled with odd, violent cartoons he drew of men carrying their eyeballs in their fists. He wanted to be a tattoo artist one day, and Crow had gone and done this without him.

"I got plans tonight, so I don't have all day to film your movies. Plus you wasted most of it getting some corny-as-hell ink on your tits."

"You got an anatomy issue," said Crow. "Because this is not my tit. It's called a chest."

"Well, whatevers," said Jed. "Tits. Chest. Morgan calls it the same thing."

Morgan. The girl whose mom was a mall psychic and part-time hairdresser. Morgan wore makeup that made her face television perfect. She was 100 percent in love with Jed, and everyone knew it, and he knew it, too. Crow heard Morgan talk a few times and it sounded like she had rocks for brains, but still, Crow had written down the things she rattled off about star signs and something called Mercury in retrograde.

"Morgan sucks," said Crow.

"Yeah, she do," said Jed and his smile was an inside joke with himself.

"Dead," Little Joey said. He skated over to them. "I got a crazy trick thing I going to try."

Jed smiled and said, "Get your camera, Crow."

Crow tried to imagine what Jed's dad might look like. Would he have the same freckle-blasted face, wet-leather smell, and lips prone to chapping?

The closest thing Jed had to a male role model was Little Joey's dad, who let Jed tag along during father and son weekends to fish for spotted bass and brim. Little Joey's father would come to their mother's house, where Little Joey and Jed both lived, and smoke cigarettes on the front porch with their mother as if they were still together. Maybe Little Joey's dad thought Jed was his son's brother and that was enough. Maybe his mother flirted the idea into Little Joey's dad's head. *The boy needs a father figure*, she might have said as she coughed strawberry-flavored smoke into his face. Little Joey's dad was a loud man with eyes that lingered too long on Crow's body.

Jed had disappeared to see his dad a lot lately. The mysterious dad picked Jed up at mysterious times and took him to do mysterious things. Crow would call the house before she came down the hill to where Jed lived and his mom would answer in her gruff voice that sweetened upon hearing who it was.

"Ain't here, honey. Gone again. I'll tell him you called."

The three of them stopped by King Tut's for greasy triangles of pizza topped with extra cheese, and somehow the camera was in Jed's hands again. Little Joey sucked Kool-Aid straight from the packet without diluting it in water. He crunched ice cubes, and Jed dared him to put hot sauce under the patch he'd started wearing to correct his wandering eye.

"Or you could snort the Kool-Aid up your nose," said Jed, "and I'll film it."

"You're not wasting film on that," said Crow.

"You need to live a little and stop pretending you're an angel," said Jed. "Let me do some directing."

Sometimes when Crow reviewed the film, she'd find random scenes of Jed flashing his nipples at the camera.

They ate their pizzas quick, hardly chewing, and left through the humid glass doors, boards under arms. The grip tape glinted against the sun. Crow suggested they skate up to the university campus, which was near empty because of summer break. The streets were vacant, so vacant it was almost eerie. The three of them looked shifty, out of place, both in age and in something else. *What was it?* It was more than the white boy rap Jed blared from a boombox in his backpack. It was more than Little Joey's eyepatch, and Crow's bowl cut and her bright white God Mark. Crow couldn't put it into words, but she felt it like a pimple beneath the skin. Or like a layer of dirt that settled on her cheeks after a day skating outside. It was something about their bodies. She wanted to imprint that feeling onto the film, that feeling of being ugly to the world.

Big oaks lined the grand university roads, and birds ate the silence with their strange songs. Jed grabbed a handful of honeysuckle and crushed it in his fist. He popped the crumpled flowers into his jaw and chewed.

"Sick," said Crow. "That's literally drenched in pesticides."

"Do I look like I give two fucks?" said Jed.

Little Joey brooded beside them, silent as always, gnawing at who-knows-what in his mind's mouth. A smile licked his lips when he heard Jed's profanity.

"You think you bad but you ain't bad," said Crow. "Stop playing."

"Two fucks still not given," said Jed.

Little Joey giggled

"Two fucks not given," repeated Little Joey.

Little Joey wiped his mouth with the back of his hand, and Crow eyed the hemp bracelet fraying around his wrist, the one Jed made himself with rope he'd picked out at a craft store.

Crow chose two places on campus where she wanted to film. First, a staircase that dashed down the front of the science building. She wanted Jed to ollie over them, maybe do a shove-it. Second, a handrail that curved along the edge of a cement structure near the student center.

She unsheathed her video camera from her backpack as if she were pulling a magic sword from a stone. Everything looked different when she peered through the camera. Above them, the sky was hot pink. She stared at the pink through the camera's eye. Blue clouds drifted across it. The temperature must have been 100 degrees. Hotter even. It brought mosquitoes and cricket croaks and a watery light that looked cool on film. The boys stripped off their shirts and Jed tried to string together a simple set around the parking lot as a warmup. Little Joey watched him with his arms crossed, lower lip stuck out.

Jed skated not so well. Bad even. It was like the better Little Joey got, the worse Jed became. Little Joey was sucking skills right from the body of his brother. Crow skated near Jed, crouched down on her board, camera to her eye, trying to get a good shot, but Jed couldn't land a trick. He threw his board into the empty pavilion. The smack of metal trucks against the ground rung out.

"Take five," said Crow.

Crow scanned the area for another place to film. An insecticide van drove down the road across from them. A few young children, who probably lived with their parents in faculty housing, raced after the van. They ran barefoot and shirtless through the green spray that painted the air. They looked like they were chasing clouds. The serrated tops of pines stood up like cut-outs of black construction paper pasted against the horizon. Clouds frothed above them. Her eyes moved to where the birds swooped and dove through the tips of those pines. She noticed the water tower.

Jed and Crow climbed it once in the middle of night. The ladder was corroded and rusted red. Jed had said *just keeping looking up*, as if to soothe Crow's fear, but she knew he needed to hear it himself, too. Her thighs shook inside her jeans. Her fingers shook around the rungs. They stayed up there for an hour, spitting off the edge, and hollering into night and flipping coins from their pockets into the sky for luck. She thought that Jed might kiss her that night, but he hadn't, and that's when she knew he never would.

"I'm peacing," Jed said. "Sorry."

"Where?" said Crow.

"None of your biz-nasty," he said.

"Your dad?" Crow said.

The word dad caught in her throat. She realized she had never said that word to him before.

"Not today, Birdy," said Jed. "I got a date with the devil."

"Okay," said Crow. "Who's the devil then?"

"Morgan's mom is reading my future in her shop. She already told me she thinks I'm probably going to be famous. A model." He shrugged. "We'll see."

Crow decided to take Little Joey out for ice cream while Jed went to have his fortune read. He wanted vanilla with real strawberries on top. He pushed his nose against the glass and watched a white girl with Caribbean hair-beading dig two perfect scoops from the Very Very 'Nilla bin. The girl smiled at them through her blue braces. She probably thought Little Joey was Crow's little brother. Crow looked down at him, ice cream already melting into the fist that held the cone, and she felt the urge to kiss the top of his dirty head. He sat in the plastic chair and licked the scoops with such care that Crow wanted to buy him another one right then and there. He stared out of the window while he licked. His pink tongue darted in and out of his mouth like he was a baby animal. Crow wondered what the hell that brain of his conjured up. He seemed like such a sketch of himself without Jed around to mimic, like a shadow with no body to fall away from.

When Crow came back from the bathroom, Little Joey had taken the ragged end of the baby tooth he carried around and was carving a pentagram into the flesh of his thigh. He had already scratched out a gun.

"What the hell you doing?" said Crow.

She grabbed the tooth from his hand, and he tried to bite her. His thigh looked raw with fresh sawing. Blood ran down to his shoes.

"What's wrong with you?"

Little Joey just stared at her and then he started to bark real low and steady. He kept barking even when she pulled him from the ice cream shop. He barked all the way home.

Jed would not tell Crow what Morgan's mom saw in her crystal ball or whatever medium mall psychics use. Then he stopped skateboarding all together. Crow began to film only Little Joey, but she didn't like the footage that came from it. It was too manic, almost violent; footage of a boy throwing himself at cement over and over again. Jed would come and observe, but he never got on the board or anything. One day, he appeared in his backyard while Crow watched Little Joey grind a waxed-up ledge, and he smelled like Axe body spray.

"You reek," said Crow, annoyed that his hair was freshly washed and even more annoyed that he wore new glasses, delicate and steel. Anything unfamiliar on him seemed to signal the end of something for her.

"Chill, dude," said Jed. "Just wanted to come out and say peace. I'm going somewhere for the weekend."

Crow walked through his room after he left and jotted down anything of interest she found. A bullet cartridge, thick as a tube of lipstick. Orange prescription bottle filled with peppermints. Envelope with his name on it but the letter inside gone.

On Sunday night, Crow waited by the bushes across the street from his house. She didn't know what she would say to Jed when he got home, but she needed to say something. She would tell him about Little Joey and how he started scribbling swastikas all over everything and how she caught him banging his head against his boxboard and how he kept scratching his eye until it bled and rode his skateboard over a lizard on purpose to kill it. She would ask him if he was spending all day with Morgan. *Morgan.* Crow wouldn't kiss Morgan. She considered it. Nah. She decided she wouldn't. It was one of many things Jed did that she wouldn't.

A red truck drove right up to Jed's house. Country music poured from the rolled down windows. Sticky chords of bluegrass and mountain sadness. It was all twang and strum. Jed made fun of anything from Appalachia. He liked music that was hard and mean. A man sat in the driver's seat. He put his forearms onto the steering wheel and leaned in. He looked like Jed would look if he were older by a couple decades and made to ride on a tractor for days. Burnt face, jowls that hung down like a pug dog. Crow got out her camera and pressed it against her eye. She did it fast. Instinct had taken over. Whirr went the film, spinning, catching the moment. She felt her God Mark itch as if something were about to happen. She watched Jed shrink against the passenger door like he didn't want to get out but like he didn't want to stay in either. The big man talked, waved a hand in front of his face as if he might snatch something from the air. When the big man laughed, his shoulders shook. He reached for something in the glove compartment and pulled out a pack of cigarettes. He shook two into his hand, stuck them in his lips, and lit them. He handed one to Jed. Jed didn't smoke. He hated his mother's smoking, the rocks it made of her voice, the smell it made of his clothes. A tightness clawed up Crow's back and settled into knots in her neck. She watched Jed close his eyes and inhale. She wanted to close her eyes, too, but she kept them open. Jed relaxed back into the seat. He smiled that lazy, sleepy, Jed smile. Both of the men did. The both of them exhaled two lines of clean blue clouds into the air. Nothing about them was different. Their smoke dissolved into nothing she could see.

Skatepark

The summer after my first year at the new school was an homage to the skateboard. Girls walked right up to the edge of the wooden ramps to watch us. Naomi came for me, but whenever I looked up after I pulled a sick trick, she was staring somewhere else, eyes caught adrift in the clouds and Orange Crush cans. Most of them got bored after a couple of hours and fled home, leaving behind smudges of pink gum on the bleachers and the smell of gardenia detergent in the breeze. I understood why they left. I would have been bored too if I were them. That summer I skated until my thighs were nothing but squiggly lines in my jeans. I lived for the sound of shove-its, 50-50 grinds, and the un-cushioned thump of wheels smacking the pavement after a kickflip.

That was the summer I met Diego. We were the only 12-year-olds brave enough to drop-in on the 20-foot half-pipe. I think it surprised him, that a girl dared to take the same risks as he did. We fell often, skidding across the rough pavement and slushing the skin on our knees. We broke ribs and napped off concussions. Raised pink moons clung to our elbows and chins. But falling didn't matter. In fact, it mostly felt good. If you could get up, it was like you were defying something.

Diego would drop in before the older BMXers with their stallions of steel. He'd sail in graceful heel-flips over the handrails on the center funbox. He was an odd, not-yet-muscled boy. His distaste for hierarchy charmed me. He smelled like Skittles. When he'd offer his candies to me, I picked out the blue ones. The sugar stung my gums like glory.

Diego had the kind of beauty I'd only ever seen on girls. His skin was the color of oiled wood. His lips were so pretty it looked like someone painted them on. One day just the two of us were left with our torn bags of candy and our sore and singing thighs. Dusk was settling and other skaters were pumping speed toward home. A clawing in my chest, because I hadn't wanted to go. Petra was on a manic upswing, and I couldn't bear the cheerful chatter, the well-thought-out meals, the bubbly laughter—sips of champagne—after every joke.

Daylight savings had just come, so the sun stayed above the horizon long after it should have. The sky was ultramarine at its edges. Almost cadmium. The color spread across the arched backs of billboards. A light explosion, Diego called it. I said it was just pollution. The orange ball setting in the sky burned and glowed and drew our eyes to it. I watched the sun as Diego offered me some Skittles and patted the pavement next to him like, *sit down?*

He started talking about his dad, boom, out of nowhere, how he was scared to go home and face him.

"It's been one of those weeks?" he said. "He's puffy, glazed over, lethargic. Kind of sweet to everyone? You know? It's a signal. Bad times around the bend."

He must have heard about my mother. Nearly everyone at school had by now. The rumor mill churned out stories as true and colorful as a fistful of Petra's pills. Maybe it made him trust me because he started saying some dark shit. His family was quite possibly more fucked up than mine. He told me about his tongue turning bloody from his father's fist and spitting a pink soup of teeth into the sink last Christmas. There was the time he saw his baby brother dangled by a small, infant leg from his parents' two-story window. *You love him more than me, don't you?* His father had shouted at his mother. A threat.

"One day he's fine, and he wants to show me how to plant broccoli sprouts in the backyard. He starts talking about moving to Hood River to buy an apple farm and shit. Then next thing I know he's throwing a chair through the back window because I left a few lemonade crystals on the counter."

I let him talk and the more he talked, the softer he got. He looked at me with these eyes that got larger and more soulful with each minute. We kept getting closer, inching our elbows toward each other, so close I could smell the Skittles on his breath. I wondered if they were the blue ones and what the blue would taste like on his tongue. I didn't know what to say, so when he kissed me I just let him. His mouth was warm as the earth. Maybe I liked it. I think I did. I think I liked it. His lips had rough flakes that softened against my mouth. I opened my eyes, and his were closed. I closed mine, too, and I pictured Naomi and wondered what it would feel like if this were her.

Then he was on top of me. His long-nailed fingers unbuttoned my jean shorts. His hands were on my just-gray cotton panties. His nails tickled and then pinched and then I had to close my eyes to concentrate and tell myself not to move. It was the first time anyone touched me there. I was surprised by how soft his hands were, how free from any hardness. He was the kind of person who cut his nails with clippers instead of eating them.

"This okay?" he whispered, his words hot in my ear.

"Yeah," I said, because maybe it was. My mouth was against his neck. A tendon tensed, and I felt it.

"Let's move behind this ramp," he said, breathing heavy. Was anyone else around? I didn't know, but the thought scared me.

"Do you know what to do?" I asked him.

"I have brothers and stuff," he told me, as if this should be reassuring, as if I should know what that meant.

I kept hoping we'd hear the sound of a board and its wheels against the pavement. Someone coming, a reason to rethink this. He laid me down on a patch of hard red dirt covered in clover and got on top of me and pulled his hair back into a ponytail. Between his legs, a half-hard thing pointed its eye at me. It was purple, so purple maybe something was wrong with it. When I began to stroke it, I was surprised by how easy it was to make him moan. It was a power I had never known. There was a pinch when he entered me, and I lost my breath.

I went home with blood in my underwear. When Petra asked what happened later that week, holding my panties like a science project over the washing machine, I told her I started my period. *Yay*, she squealed, pronouncing me woman. I took the tampons she bought me and dipped them in cups of water, awed at how far the cotton could expand.

The next week at school, Diego's eyes went through me like wind. There was a chill between us that could have been indifference. Diego never said hi, but grunted greetings if we occupied the same enclosed spaces at school. It was like I had begun dressing in camouflage. I faded into the wallpaper. I went to the skatepark exactly four more times after that night. Then I stopped going.

"You must be growing up," Petra said.

And I just nodded like, yeah.

Transplant

My back is to to the door when Larnie B opens it, but I see her anyway. I've tried to arrange my hair so she can't notice the second set of eyes implanted into the back of my skull. For the most part, it works. I don't think Larnie B has any idea, and this being our first date I'm not going to say a thing.

Tate's Seafood is near empty at this hour. It's too early for dinner, barely 5 p.m. I secured a table near the window and a basket of yeast rolls for us to split. Larnie B is just as cute as her Tinder pic promised. Now I regret using my best photo with that misleading filter. I should have listened when Myrtle said "always use a picture that's not your favorite. The last thing you want is a date from the internet showing up and thinking you're uglier than she expected."

"Not from here, huh? Just passing through?" I ask.

I suck down my sweet tea. It's like gasoline firing up my blood, kickstarting my heart. Larnie B says *uh huh*. She's some kind of big-time journalist come down from Washington DC to report on our elections. Tate's Seafood is the best restaurant in town, right on the river with floor-to-ceiling windows. No one has contracted any kind of food poisoning from eating anything on the menu.

"We got some crazy gubernatorial candidate now, huh?" I say. "I want you to know that I know. I want you to know I believe the women who say he kept them caged in his basement for 11 months in the 1980s."

Larnie B nods. She raises an eyebrow that means: *it's crazy as all hell.* We both know Alabama will elect this man to office, but I need her to see that I'm different than other folks here. Outside the sky is changing colors. The sun is hot oil burning down the horizon, and its blood is orange. If there's one thing Alabama is good for, it's gruesome sunsets.

"Look," Larnie B says. "I'm reserving judgments. I'm just here to get the facts."

"You mean the fake news?" I smile. I make gotcha guns with my fingers and fire them right at her. "The guy's a frigging nut job. We both know it."

"So, what's good here?" says Larnie B.

I see she's an expert at changing the topic. Noted, Larnie B, noted.

"I'll die if I eat another plate of barbecue or cheese grits," she says.

She talks like someone from the TV. The menu glistens in her hand, all laminate and chicken grease. Her blouse is unbuttoned at the top. I wonder why she went on this date with me, Larnie B from the big city. My eyes fall to the smooth, sun-freckled skin that her blouse would usually cover. I think *damn, Larnie B.*

"The catfish," I say. "It tastes like fried butter. Swear to God."

Larnie B laughs, a pure, pleasing shriek. She thinks I'm cute. I got that kind of farmer look that might be exotic to city ladies. I've been compared to a horse. My hair is a mane cascading down my shoulders.

"I'll take it," she says. "The catfish."

I see the waiter behind us pocket a pack of sweetener from table 10. I see it with my implanted eyes, so I see it fuzzy. He could just be collecting his tips. Maybe wiping the surface down. He could be brandishing a fork to use as a weapon.

Implanted eyes don't work like normal ones. Implanted eyes broadcast reality like a TV set on the fritz: all crackle and snow. They show the world in black and white and mostly just reveal shadows and shapes, but I've learned to make out things pretty accurately. Still, it's distracting. I close my implanted eyes so I can focus on the moment in front of me. *On Larnie B.* Larnie B asks about my job, and I start talking about Silas and our jewelry making business. I talk about the business like it's something I do and not a dream never realized. I talk like Silas is still alive. I show Larnie B the bracelet he made out of invertebrate fossils. The pygmy squirrel skull I wear as a brooch.

"Wow," she says. Larnie B's tongue slides across her lips. Maybe she's licking them for me, to be suggestive about sex, or maybe her lips are chapped and need a wipe down. It's hard to discern what's what sometimes.

"That's, um," she says. "That's original."

"Oh, don't be too impressed," I say. "It's nothing you couldn't make yourself with hot glue."

Our waiter comes to take our catfish order. He's got a gun holster on his belt filled with butter knives. Larnie B eyes the holster. Maybe that detail will find its way into the piece she's writing. With her near, I'm noticing things I never had before. The framed photographs of Alabama football players throughout the decades. They used to wear leather helmets! The taxidermy raccoon nailed above the bathroom door. The buck antlers turned into candle holders for our table. The waiter's camouflage pants.

"Are you ever afraid someone's going to shoot you like they did that journalist on TV?" I ask. "I mean really. Being a public figure seems dangerous."

"No," Larnie B says. The way she says it, I believe her. It doesn't seem like she's given that one thought. "I'm not exactly a public figure. I just write for the internet. You know, like blogs?"

"Well, you should be afraid. Let's look at the facts," I say. A shadow flaps through my posterior vision. Probably a stray child on the roam. "People are born mean. Scheming. There's no telling how many dead bodies are sleeping under that lake out there. There aren't enough eyes in the world to catch all the crime. Aren't enough reporters to report it either."

Outside the lake looks still as glass, the dock a stable, unmoving thing, but I know it sways with the water. Things aren't what they seem. I wonder if they have lakes like this in DC, sunsets like this anywhere else in the world. Larnie B turns her head to watch the lake. Her movement sends a shiver through me. It's like I'm a director, and she is my play. I told Larnie B to look, and she did. I said here's a fear, and it became one.

I earned my new set of eyes. I held them in my hands, two globules of wet heat, the same feeling and texture as skinned grapes and heard them say: *home*. The car crash had been horrible, a true terror. Now Silas was gone, but his eyes made it out. When I woke up on my back, flung from the seat of the Dodge Durango and onto that cruel asphalt gone cold with the night, Silas was still strapped in. He was upside down, held into place by the seat belt and dead. Music played from the speakers like it thought we were still driving. Now Silas's eyes are blinking in the back of my head. It's better than having an angel. Silas isn't just watching over me; he's literally watching for me.

The first time I saw Silas's eyes, I knew I'd love them forever. They lived in his face then, and there was no reason to think they wouldn't stay there always. Silas called them sunflower eyes because of the way his irises were ringed in golden bands like the uneven petals of a flower.

"Don't fret so much," Silas told me after the mass shooting in Devil's Ridge, not far from where we lived.

I was washing new cracks into my hands from worry. The skin split open at the knuckles. I kept thinking there were still germs on my skin. How could there not be? I touched the faucet after washing and faucets were smothered in germs. So many germs. It was impossible to understand how anyone stayed alive at all.

"You know," Silas told me. "I've never met anyone so terrified to die."

He shook his head, that Silas head bristling with a fat orange bouffant. He pulled at the end of his beard, thick and always growing. He was so still alive then. At the river, Silas waded knee-deep into the rapids. His sunflower eyes combed the water. He plunged his hand in to dig for shark teeth hidden in the silt bottom. Silas collected the teeth for his jewelry making. A rabbit paw swung from the lobe of his left ear.

"The shark teeth in this river is proof," he said. "That things are always changing, that the very ground we're standing on used to be an ocean."

I didn't want to get caught in one of those swift river rapids. They were like death traps. I spread out and tanned on a slab of rock instead. I lathered SPF 75 over every inch of skin. A mole on my stomach stopped me. *Hello, hotdog-shaped mole with a curl of black hair.* I'd heard something about mole hairs. They either signaled health or cancer. I couldn't remember which. My fingers pinched at the mole and examined it close. Down the river, past the bend, a rope swing hung from the high branch of a tree. A group of teenagers took turns using it to slingshot their bodies into the currents. Their grunts had the ominous tenor of boys who congregate together. Even their splashes sounded violent. Each time they yelled, I jerked my head in their direction, sure that one of them had drowned or been carted down the stream by a renegade current.

"Found another," said Silas.

He held up a beautiful black curve, sharp as a hunger pang. I thought we'd have a million more afternoons like that one. The quality of light was near perfect, like something from a southern song.

"Hey," Silas said. "Live a little. Come get in the river. I'm watching you."

Larnie B listens as I tell her about Silas. My hands itch to be disinfected. I can feel the germs crawl across them. The story makes them dirty. I squirt a blob of hand sanitizer onto the open flakes of palm skin and rub it in.

I tell Larnie B how we were driving home listening to "Bittersweet Symphony" by the Verve when it happened.

"Swear to God," I say. "You know? The theme song to *Cruel Intentions*."

"Oh, I know it," says Larnie B. "Used to blast it with the windows down."

I nodded. We aren't so different after all.

"A white wolf ran into the middle of the road. A sign. Straight from nowhere."

"A sign of what?" Larnie B asks.

"Well," I say. "I haven't really thought that far into it. All I know is it was a sign."

Her chin rests on her fist, and she's really looking at me. This woman from faraway is so close. She's not as pretty as I once thought. Her genes stutter. I see it in that short neck, droopy earlobes, bulb of a nose. I see it now, and it relieves me like maybe I can have her after all. These flaws make her accessible. Wet stinging on my cheeks. I'm not sure what's happening. I might be crying. I shove a forkful of catfish into my mouth. Hot butter. The texture is hot breaded butter. A thing that once lived just like me, just like Silas, is now in my mouth, and I'm masticating it. I wonder what piece is in my mouth right this second. Maybe the muscle near the spine. Or the sweet meat behind the dorsal fin that helped it move. I wonder what they do with catfish eyes. Another blob lumbers behind me, in and out of my vision. My implanted eyes say look. Through the static, I can't tell what it is: friend or enemy, child or mass shooter. It could be anything.

I grab a bottle of wine from my truck and take Larnie B on a walk through the well-trod path near the restaurant. She says the most shocking thing isn't that people in this state don't believe the women who said the candidate kept them in his basement for years. What Larnie B finds odd is that the people here say that even if the candidate did keep the girls in his basement, that's okay. They'll vote for him anyway. They believe in redemption, and the candidate is an evangelical. Who are they not to forgive him when God already has? They say, look at the girls, such healthy and well-adjusted adults. Maybe the time in his basement did them good. Maybe he took care of them. Maybe he saved them. Maybe he saw the girls at the ice cream shop, those little lost lambs in need of guidance, and took them so he could turn them toward Jesus and release them back into the world to spread God's word.

That's what the people say.

The pine trees weep, and a strong wind brings their needles down. We're a couple glasses of pinot noir deep when we start to have casual sex right there on the ground. As we're making out, my implanted eyes see a shape appear above us, a ruffle in the branches. My eyes can't tell what it is yet but I see falling.

"Watch out," I say.

I roll Larnie B out of the way. I'm just in time because a snake drops right on the ground where we were. It's a small garden snake, but we both scream. Its oil-black body slithers away. I feel like I'm standing at the edge of a cliff about to jump off into the water. My heart pumps that fast.

"God," Larnie B says. "That could have fallen right on me."

"But it didn't," I say. "We got away just in time."

Boy
Box

In her diary, Francis writes encouragement, suggestions for bettering her life. Tonight she scribbles: Less cautious! Be the man! Speak up!

Her name: the thing *Francis* thanks God for above all else. Signing Francis to the end of an email does not pin one down: androgynous, gender neutral. Frank, the most popular nickname for Francis, denotes boy. *Frank*. She says it out loud. She tries it on. To the mirror, she says, *Frank*. Extends a palm. She gives a turn for her reflection.

Francis likes to walk around topless in just underwear, but she only does it when the fathers aren't home. Tonight's a night like this: fatherless. Men gone. Shirt off. Francis squeezes her right nipple and studies it. A little fatter than a boy. The roots of something lie inside. The tissue wants to soften and bloom. She squeezes hard enough to hurt her eyes. More here today than yesterday even. This is worrisome.

The cage in her fathers' bedchamber is off limits, but when the dads don't hang around, Francis likes to sit inside of it. A blanket is draped over the cage to make it look like furniture, nice décor, just part of the apartment, but Francis wasn't born yesterday. She knows the fathers' cage is for fucking. For fucking each other, but also for fucking Gideon and Rex, men who aren't her fathers, men they met on the internet, men they met at a bar.

Francis sits in the cage and pulls at the strands of her long-haired head. She spreads out her stash of riot grrrl zines. The covergrrrl on Francis's beloved zine does not have long locks but a half-shaved skull dyed black and a tattoo of a unicorn eating a shark on her neck. The girl screams into a microphone. Cartoon sweat pings off her head. Francis can feel the words drip down her spine. *I just wanna-I just wanna-I just wanna fee-fee-eeee-feeel you!* This covergrrrl is from the band Sunday Sex. Sunday Sex sings about period blood and giving head. Francis has experienced neither of these, but she gets the idea.

Her zines: the best things she owns. Multi-colored universes stapled together with canvas, felt, and computer paper. She'll never meet who made them, but she feels somehow connected to them. The zines came to her by way of Crane's older sister, Kit. They were not a gift. Francis stole them. *Kit.* Just thinking her name makes Francis want to pop every knuckle on her left hand. Kit's hair is as bright as Listerine, her eye makeup smudged just enough to make her look a little tired all the time. Her bones are big, and her breasts are bigger than any Francis has seen in real life. She thinks of Kit's neck, how warm it must be, how it must smell yeasty like the bread

Crane's father bakes on the weekends. Francis slips her hand under
the elastic of her boxer shorts. Her head clunks against the cage
behind her. *Kit.*

A rustle at the door sends Francis to her feet. She clamors from
the cage and throws the fancy covering back over it. Two at a time
steps take her to her room. She puts on a shirt and arranges herself,
slightly out of breath, on her bed with her Sunday Sex zine open
before her. The footfalls belong to Father First, lighter in his move-
ments that Father Second. A two-knuckle knock on the door.

"Honey?" he says. "Can I come in?"

"Enter the chamber, sir," she says.

"How do I look?" He holds his hands out from his side and gives
a turn. His voice is warm, his eyes two slices of summer in the middle of a fake-tan face. All right angles. He's acquired a new hardness
from a recent diet of bunless bison burgers.

"Tired," says Francis. "You need a shave."

"I feel tired," he admits.

"Me too."

"Lucky girl. You get to stay in."

"Get to?" says Francis.

"Come to the loo and help me shave the back of my neck. Will
you?"

The lotion she lathers into his skin smells like fallen pines. She
touches the long tendons on his neck. The desire to climb onto his
back and sit on his shoulders overwhelms her. She likes the sound of
the blade cutting stubble and the pink drawn up by the razor's teeth.
On the tips of her toes to get it all, the rough patches gone, she

pats away the small hairs and leftover cream with a towel. Although Francis doesn't share a single gene with either dad, Father First's face is eerily like her own. No one doubts she is his daughter.

A missed patch of stubble stands near his starched collar. When Francis takes the blade to it, she draws a speck of blood. The cut is deep, and more red threatens to rise and run. He exhales hard. A muscle twitches under his skin. Francis licks her thumb and presses the spot good and hard.

"All done," she says.

"Did you get me?" he asks, trying to find the cut.

"Um," she says. "Kinda."

He turns. *Smiles.*

"Not a big deal. You always do the best job. Like a pro."

"Whatever. It's easy," says Francis.

"How's that friend of yours, Crane?" he says this as he studies his temples in the mirror, pushes at a patch of gray rising up in his black curls. "Now that's an odd fellow."

"No odder than me."

"Than I."

Father First turns the corners of his mouth to a frown. His eyes study his body, the accumulated age.

"Why is everything so much harder for you, honey? You've got to learn to lighten up. Smile more, that sort of thing."

"Crane's not my boyfriend by the way. He's my boy comma friend."

"Did I say he was your boyfriend?"

Father First tucks a hand into his pocket and directs his attention to Francis. He isn't looking at her, but through her, flipping the catalog of memories: the adoption center, Montessori daycare, *Lion King*-themed pool parties, everything he thought she needed always. Youth is wasted on the young and all that.

"I'm going to go read," says Francis. "I won't wait up for you."

"Hey. Brunch in the a.m.? Choco pancakes? Anything you like."

Francis checks the bus schedule on her phone, but nothing is coming for another two hours. She needs to get there faster, which is where her legs come in. Tonight, Francis heeds her own advice: *less cautious*. The Fathers will not notice she is gone. They will not come and crack the door to check on her upon their return. They will retire to the upstairs where they will bind themselves in saran wrap. She does not bother making the covers look occupied, as she has observed teens do on TV. All she needs is to find an outfit that isn't 100% nerd or 99% goody-good. She takes a gray sweater and cuts off the sleeves. She scissors three slashes over the chest. She decorates it with buttons she bought at Walmart and pulls on her red running sneakers. She wraps a piece of black panty hose around her wrist. Her cell buzzes in her back pocket. Crane's pic flashes on the screen.

"Yo ho," she says into the speaker.

"I'm leaving in T minus 10," says Crane.

"I don't even know what that means," says Francis as she turns to check how the fresh slashes look from all angles.

"Time till launch. 10 minutes till launch," says Crane, and she can picture him rolling his eyes.

"Ok, smarts, sounds good. See you in T."

"That's wrong. You're using the phrase wrong on purpose."

"Should I wear my purple shirt or? I dunno. I just did this thing where I cut the sleeves off my favorite sweater. What are you wearing?"

"Just a thing. I'm wearing pants. The usual uniform."

"Uh-huh. Is Kit around? What's she wearing? Something black?"

Crane empties his lungs into the receiver.

"Who cares?" he asks.

"Ok, weirdo," Francis says. "I'm letting you go now. Father is on his way out. I can hear him pocketing twelve handfuls of condoms into his pants as we speak. See you in T minus 10. Or whatever."

"Whatever," says Crane. "See. You. Then."

They disconnect. Francis clips in a septum ring. She stays in her room for a whole fifteen minutes after Father First leaves the house, just making sure. Two miles to the venue. She takes off at a slow pace for the show. It's the kind of night with the day still in it. Pink blurs the edges of the black sky. A couple of blocks away, Francis feels the chug chug chug of Sunday Sex inside her chest. She stops and rips a sprig of lavender from a bush. She rubs it over her face and arms, shoves it inside her training bra.

A lilac-haired boy leans against a bike rack, thank God. She walks up to him, and they touch their fists together. She can see Kit's face inside Crane's. The edges of the mouth. The hairline. They share blood. That much is obvious. She must be here. Somewhere. Francis loops her arm through Crane's: the one body she is comfortable touching. Together they are more. The new acne drug Crane is taking makes him more anxious than usual, but the craters on his cheeks are less. No new sores. Nothing picked or aflame on his face. Self-confidence can't be far off.

They open the door, break the borders of the venue, and become part of the swarm. Francis fights the urge to cover her ears. It's so loud. But no one else seems to notice. The sound is all the way inside of her, thumping and bumping like a mosh pit. The song tunnels through the air. Francis studies a condom stuck to the floor and imagines the penis it once went on. Crane pulls away, his sticky body no longer part of hers.

"Lot of people," says Francis.

"Yup," says Crane. "That's why they call it a party."

"Where's your sister anyway? She playing tonight? I have something to give her."

Crane puts his hands on his hips.

"Give her?" he says.

"Like a thing. I have a thing."

"She's somewhere. But what do you have to give her?" He asks.

Maybe, Francis thinks, Crane is jealous.

"Let's get a drink! A drink!" Francis says. "Coca-Cola with vodka?"

Crane pulls a flask from his back pocket and tips it toward her.

"You can't order anything. You look prepubescent."

"Fuck you, man," Francis says, but she takes the flask anyway.

Warmth slips into her throat. It stings her awake. When she drinks, the ringing in her ears gets less loud.

"She's there," says Francis, nudging Crane.

"So?"

Kit sits under an arc of wheat-pasted posters not unlike the images from the zines in her room. Someone in a hunting cap whispers in Kit's ear, but it doesn't change her expression. Bored. Kit looks bored. The whole world bores her. Her eyes find Francis and settle. Kit's gaze bends Francis's breath. It bends her knees. There is something frightening about the way Kit can keep looking without blinking. She raises her glass at Crane and Francis.

"She wants to talk to you," Francis says to Crane. "Let's go say hi."

"Seriously? What is wrong with you? She's fucked up right now, and I doubt she even recognizes me, much less wants to say hi."

"I think she does. I think she is trying to get our attention," says Francis.

"She doesn't even know your name. She keeps calling you Frank."

"She does? Really?"

"Stop smiling," says Crane. "That's not your name."

"Nothing."

"What?" says Crane, yelling over the music.

"Nevermind!"

"What?"

Francis turns from Crane to the bench where Kit was sitting, but it's empty. She scans the room and she spots her: green hair going toward the toilets.

"I've got to pee," Francis says and points at her crotch.

"Hey," says Crane. "Be careful. She's no one you should trust."

Francis steps to the end of the line, behind a girl with pigtails and a lower back piercing. She's annoyed at Crane again. He's so paranoid. But Francis gets why. She really does. She knows Crane is afraid of his sister for the same reasons she's drawn to her. Kit's unpredictable. She's the kind of person that can change you. The air around Kit crackles like she's tearing it open.

Someone stuck a rod of nag champa in a vent above the sink, and an inch is ready to fall off onto the liquid smeared tile. Kit emerges from her stall, sucking on a lollipop and shouting hysterics at her cellphone. Everyone in the bathroom stops what they're doing to watch. She doesn't wipe away the mascara blackening her cheeks. The music from the concert hall swings through Francis. It makes her want to punch the air with her fist. She hates all of these bodies so close to her, the wet arm sweat, the collective breathing. She can't hear what Kit is so upset about, even when Kit walks directly in front of her, close enough for Francis to grab.

Cold fingers wrap around Francis's wrist. Kit's fingers. Her nails are colored in with black marker. Kit shakes her head at Francis, still holding onto her wrist, as if the two of them are in on something together, as if Francis is listening in on the phone call, too. Kit's eyes glisten, wet as the bathroom tiles. She mouths *Douchewad* and hangs up her phone. A moment of stillness holds them together, maybe a thousand seconds. Kit softens, like Francis is a friend she hasn't seen in years, like she really sees her. Then she begins to choke on her lollipop. Kit stomps her feet and brings her hands to her neck. Her face is red. Her face is purple.

"Does anyone know CPR?" yells the girl next to Francis.

Kit looks at Francis and mouths the word *Frank*, and something inside of Francis says *yes*. Francis is a babysitter, trained in first aid. She steps behind Kit, wraps her arms around the torso she's dreamed of touching and gives a hard abdominal thrust. Kit is in her arms. There is the neck she wanted to smell, right against her nose. It smells like metal. It smells like girl. The Heimlich maneuver works. Kits shoots a candy shard across the room. Her airway clears. Francis wonders what it must feel like, to choke like that and then experience the release.

Kit stumbles toward Francis. Her lipstick is smeared down to her chin. Kit stares at her, mouth open and panting. She reaches out and places a palm on each of Francis's cheeks like her face is something precious to behold. Kit kisses her. Kit kisses her like she's hungry. She leans her body into Francis and pushes her into the bathroom wall where she grinds against her thigh and moans in her ear. Francis slides her palms into Kit's back pockets. Kit's breath tastes sour and undelicious, but Francis doesn't mind. She doesn't mind the people around them watching. She likes the tongue that's licking her, the rough wet of it, not unlike a dog. Kit runs a hand through her hair, and it's a thrill, the way the sharpness of it travels to her hips. The kiss ends without warning. Kit turns to leave, pushes back through the bathroom line, through the bodies. And Francis knows to follow.

The air outside steams. Francis has to remind herself to breathe. Her horoscope sign is two fish swimming in opposite directions. She's got it henna-tattooed on her ankle, and she feels the tattoo itch as if those two fish are channeling her. One wants to swim inside to find Crane, the other wants to follow Kit anywhere she'll lead. Kit burrows her eyes into Francis's face as if she can see under her skin, peel back the plump girl cheeks, excavate some deeper meaning.

"What the fuck, Frank. What the fuck was that? You're like a doctor? A lifeguard? You saved my life!"

Francis works hard not to smile. The comment is a trophy Francis puts on a shelf inside her chest. The trophy gleams. Kit hiccups into the falling night and keeps leering at Francis.

"What was that? In there? The thing you did?"

"It's called the Heimlich maneuver," says Francis. She shrugs like *no big deal.*

"You know what? You're a smart kid, and we need smart kids hanging around. I bet you study. Do you study?"

"Kind of," says Francis. "But only because I want good grades."

"Ha! You're a toddler. I forgot. You're a frigging toddler. In middle school!"

Francis says, "Can you keep a secret?"

"Not really," says Kit.

"I want to be in a band. Like you. I've been practicing the drums. I think I'm getting okay. Kind of good."

Kit sucks on her lips and looks bored.

"What do you mean?" asks Kit. "By kind of good? What the hell is kind of good?"

"Well, I was thinking you could maybe. Um. Recommend some tips to get better or whatever."

Francis imagines a practice session in Kit's garage. She pictures Kit behind her working Francis's arms, showing her what to beat and when. Kit's interest slides to the hangnail on her finger. Francis closes her eyes so she won't have to see Kit not pay attention. *Don't fuck it up*, Francis tells herself. *This is your shot.*

"It doesn't work like that," Kit says. "You just gotta play. Just do it, Frank."

"Oh," says Francis. "Well okay."

Kit picks up a broken beer bottle from the ground. She stares at the ragged edge like it's beautiful, a rare instrument, then cuts her hand wide open. She holds out her bleeding hand to Francis like she should take it.

"I want to see what kind of homo you are, Frank," says Kit. "Show me what you're made of."

"What," says Francis.

"Do it, Frank. Make a cut. A little tear. Let your insides out. Let me see you."

Francis shakes her head. Kit talks with such authority it sounds like every sentence could be framed and hung up on a wall. It seems crazy not to follow her lead. She's so bold. Francis feels her palm pound and throb as if it's already been cut open.

"I can't," Francis says. "I can't. It's. That's like a broken bottle."

"Do it, Frank."

Kit licks the blood from her palm. Then the blood is on her lips, the lips Francis kissed.

Francis looks around like the answer is somewhere nearby, in the air. Kit's attention smolders. A hot blade of iron like the kind that brands. It fumes.

"Fucking try it, Frank. Just do it. Man up."

Kit smiles. Her gums are not healthy. They are very red. Kit grabs Francis's palm and slices an identical line right down the center, over the cracks that Father First once read her fortune from. She splits the lifeline he said was so long. Kit breaks it with the bottle, tears right through it. Francis likes the pain. It tightens her jaw. Pain, she realizes, feels good.

"Ow," says Francis, but her voice is different. It's low and mean.

"You've got to come with me, kid. The dudes are not going to fucking believe it. You're so fucking cute. You're so fucking weird!"

"Where are we going?" asks Francis on the way to Kit's van, but Kit is already on her phone, texting someone, laughing. In her chest, someone is singing, but she can't understand the words.

"I have to say goodbye to Crane. He is going to wonder where I went."

"Look, Frank. NBD. Crane is a big boy. He's got this handled. Let him get a little wild in there. Shake it up."

"But where are you taking me?"

Frances buckles her seatbelt, aware of the vodka-tinged kiss from earlier and the slur that blends the end of Kit's words.

Kit holds her finger to the volume dial until the whole car is packed with noise and bass, and Francis can't tell the difference between what's beating inside of her and out. She pushes her foot into an invisible brake on the van floor, hoping for Kit to slow down on the curves, at red lights, in the woods. They drive out of the familiar into a park where it's only dark. Kit's eyes press forward, and Francis searches for Crane in her features. She needs to see him in there, to make her feel a little less alone, to make her feel like this isn't dangerous, but just another night drive to smoke cigarettes, sip dandelion beer, practice kissing on your best friend.

Acknowledgements

My deepest gratitude to my parents, Carmen Hudson and Jerry Hudson.

Special thanks to those who have read these stories along the way: Chelsea Bieker (my wolf wife and forever friend), T Kira Madden, Jamie Carr, Daniel Cecil, Kate Jayroe, and Jessica F. Walter.

Thank you to Maaike Muntinga, whose light, love, and wisdom I cherish.

I am forever grateful for the wisdom and guidance I received from my teachers and mentors over the years: Leni Zumas, Charles D'Ambrosio, Tom Bissell, Jon Raymond, Rachel Kushner, Alexander Chee, Bret Lott, and Anthony Varallo.

Thank you to the Fulbright Program, Portland State University's Creative Writing Department, Caldera Arts, the Dickinson House, the Tin House Summer Workshop, and the Vermont Studio Center, for providing me with the time and space to write.

Big thank you to Elena Kendall-Arana for your incredible photographs. And to Jess Vande Werken, you talented designer.

Much gratitude and thanks to my brilliant agent, Monika Woods.

Thank you to Kevin Sampsell, for believing in my writing and publishing these stories. And to Bianca Flores, Tyler Meese, and Jessie Carver for their work on this book.

Thank you to the people and places that published earlier versions of these stories: *Tin House, Lit Hub,* the wonderful women at *No Tokens,* Amanda Goldblatt at *Hobart,* Kait Heacock at *Joyland,* Tobias Carroll at *Vol. 1 Brooklyn,* Madeleine Maillet at *Cosmonauts Avenue,* Mensah Demary at *Catapult,* and Kodiak Armstrong at *Pacifica.*

About the Author

Genevieve Hudson is the author of *A Little in Love with Everyone* (Fiction Advocate, 2018). Her writing has been published in *Catapult, Hobart, Tin House* online, *Joyland, Vol.1 Brooklyn, No Tokens, Bitch, The Rumpus, The Collagist*, and other places. Her work has been supported by the Fulbright Program, the Tin House Summer Workshop, and artist residencies at the Dickinson House, Caldera Arts, and the Vermont Studio Center. She received an MFA in creative writing from Portland State University, where she occasionally teaches fiction writing and gender studies courses. She lives in Amsterdam.

Read more about her at www.genevievehudsonwriter.com

CPSIA information can be obtained
at www.ICGtesting.com
Printed in the USA
FSHW021601281118
54099FS